THE KEY'S REFLECTION

MICHAEL J. PIATT

Piatt BOOKS

Backlight the image pairs throughout this book and
view them through the paper.

Dedicated to the next generation.
May they see life from many perspectives.

TABLE OF CONTENTS

Diyton Theater Advisor ~ 1

Returning The Key ~ 9

The Two Boys Meet ~ 15

This Key Is Special ~ 27

Soccer Tryouts ~ 39

The Origin Of Keys ~ 53

The Glass Table ~ 67

Changes In Sharefield ~ 83

The Community Unites ~ 111

Investigating The Key ~ 147

The Search ~ 157

Difficult Decisions ~ 177

One Too Many Strange Clues ~ 197

Disaster In The Making ~ 231

The Key's Magic ~ 271

The Key's True Value ~ 283

Author ~ 291

PROLOGUE

As Lucas woke up, his hand instinctively reached for the key resting on his nightstand. But what he saw left him frozen. A surge of bewildering anxiety momentarily numbed his senses. There, on the key, appeared an image of a stack of medical books.

As his trembling fingers turned the key over, its dark side caught the glint of light. At once, its reflection transported him somewhere new. His surroundings transformed into the sterile halls of a hospital – scenes from his time as a patient flooded his mind. That is the image he saw in the key.

This was to become a common occurrence for the obscure key that Lucas always kept in his pocket. The key held within it the power to unveil unimaginable visions that saved life and ultimately shaped his world and that of his friends forever.

I

DIYTON THEATER ADVISOR

Lucas was wrapping up his tenth-grade year at Diyton South Side, one of the three high schools in Diyton. His family had recently moved to the area from out of state.

Blessed with keen reflexes, athletic build, and a size that belied his age, Lucas excelled in soccer since the third grade. His prowess on the field garnered him acclaim, and he looked forward to joining a new select summer league and forging new friendships as soon as tryouts began. With the spring theater production at Diyton South Side fast approaching, Lucas found himself drawn to the bustling preparations. That was the traditional marker of summer fast approaching.

Though somewhat shy and reserved, he happily volunteered to work backstage, much upon the insistence of cast members. The props for this year's presentation included several massive pieces of furniture. Lucas was well suited to move pieces around quickly behind the scenes, given his strength and coordination.

However, the theater program at Diyton South Side was struggling. It lacked the guidance of a seasoned director like Ms. Brock from Sharefield Central High School, ten miles from Diyton. In an effort to rejuvenate the Diyton South Side program, Ms. Brock had been invited to conduct a one-day seminar on small-scale theater production techniques. She had prepared to speak to the Diyton organization about the use of symbolic props in theater production for enhanced audience engagement.

That seminar was scheduled to take place just a couple of weeks before the Diyton South Side spring program. Ms. Brock was eager to impart her knowledge and inspire the budding artists using the experiences she had picked up from her brother Jimmy during Sharefield Central High's recent performance of *The Caribbean Adventure*.

The fall production of *The Caribbean Adventure* had been an enormous success for the Sharefield Central High School theater program. Everyone in the Sharefield Gang participated this year.

The gang was a close-knit group of friends, now near the end of the tenth grade. They had been childhood friends who went to the same school year after year.

Kim, a natural-born leader, stood out among her friends. and her infectious enthusiasm spurred the group to action.

Lucia's analytical mind, on the other hand, was more about offering great insights. Chelsea, the newest addition to the gang, brought a fresh perspective. She had moved into the Sharefield school district a year ago. Her dad had taught her about innovative technologies all her life. Earlier this year, she inspired the gang to take an interest in artificial intelligence and virtual reality through her father's job connections.

Dion, like Kim, possessed leadership qualities. Everyone respected him and his daring spirit. Nate was a loyal friend whose thirst for knowledge drove him to tackle any challenge head-on and Anthony's blend of humor would puzzle anyone to imagine that he had a deep, pensive side to him. He liked questioning the way people behaved with tremendous insight.

In addition to the six, there was Victor. He was a steadfast friend who had moved away at the beginning of the school year but remained connected to the gang through social media and occasional phone calls. Victor's organizational skills and meticulous attention to detail made him stand out from the crowd.

Everyone in the gang, including Victor, who had helped write part of the manuscript for *The Caribbean Adventure* before moving out of state, participated in the Sharefield production. Pouring their hearts into the performance, the students left a lasting impression on the small town of Sharefield.

Ms. Brock wanted to share the value of teamwork and a clear sense of direction toward a common goal. In her mind, these concepts were of utmost importance, especially for this neighboring school. She also intended to discuss the idea of using a special prop within the production to generate excitement, support a common theme, and create a sense of enchantment. She intended to carry the key with her that had played a pivotal role in the past few performances at Central High. That prop had imaginary magical powers and she was quite proud of the impact the key had on the audience, as well as the performers themselves.

Little did Ms. Brock know the influence of similar keys, both real and virtual, had shaped the lives of the members of the Sharefield gang in profound ways over the past two years. Her iconic key had been instrumental in Central High's make-believe world of theater. It had guided the storyline and entertained the audience. Similarly, for the Sharefield Gang, one magic key or another had been a major force in their lives time and again.

On the day of her presentation at Diyton South Side, Ms. Brock tossed her key into the outside pocket of her purse and headed off to the school.

The program included a theater workshop for the students and faculty, a session on how to audition and rehearse for a part, prop construction techniques, background settings, and so forth. The day culminated in a forty-five-minute presentation by Ms. Brock on the use of a special icon, such as a key, to enhance a theater performance and provide a visual symbol for the audience to remember throughout the presentation and beyond.

During her presentation, Ms. Brock held the key aloft, raising it high above her head for everyone to see. She recounted its role in the past performances of both *The Script* from the year before and *The Caribbean Adventure* from this year's Sharefield theater presentation. She urged the Diyton theater group to adopt a similar symbol for their next production to enhance their future performances.

Her message was embraced quite well. In fact, the students bombarded her with questions and accolades long after the presentation had ended. She graciously accepted the appreciation of the Diyton theater department, departing with warm goodbyes and hearty wishes for all upcoming performances, which she promised to attend.

In her haste to return home for other important commitments, Ms. Brock inadvertently lost the key on her way home. As she paraded down the hallway in high heels, her purse swung from one side to the other. The key worked its way toward the edge of the pocket with each step she took before it fell onto the hallway floor outside the music room.

Students inside were practicing their instruments. Their music drowned out the noise of her brass key hitting the linoleum floor of the school hallway as it bounced several times and landed off to one side.

After the workshop, most students at Diyton South Side were dismissed for the day. They picked up the needed books from their lockers and exited the front entrance of the school. The teachers stayed behind for a short recap of the day's events.

Meanwhile, Lucas was walking down the back hallway toward the rear doors to meet up with his soccer buddies for practice drills in the field behind the school. As he strolled through the hall toward the rear door, he stumbled upon the gold-colored key just lying there on the floor in front of the music room. Surprised, he thought to himself, *This must be the key that Ms. Brock used in her presentation. I need to return it to her.* He immediately picked it up.

As he continued toward the exit, he looked at the key closely. Lucas came to appreciate just how intricate and beautiful it was. The scroll detail on the face was incredible. It was a fine piece of workmanship. He began grappling with conflicting emotions. He thought, *I really like this key and would love to have one of my own to keep.* Yet he knew that he should return it. For the time being, he stuck it in his pocket and went off to the soccer field.

Upon arriving at her home, Ms. Brock noticed that the front pocket of her purse was unzipped and the key was missing. Panicking, she checked everywhere in her bag, but it was not to be found. She focused hard and distinctly remembered putting the key into that pocket on the front of her purse.

What could have happened to it? she thought.

The next morning, she called the principal at Diyton South Side to see if anyone had found the key. The principal said there had been no reports of it but promised to make an announcement the following morning to all students and teachers.

Lucas was in homeroom that morning and listened intently to the announcement. The key was still tucked away in his pocket. He now faced a moral dilemma.

Thinking about it some more, he realized that it was a double-edged key, figuratively speaking. Should he come forward and return the key, risking the loss of something he had grown attached to? Or should he keep silent and continue to enjoy the secret thrill of possessing such a coveted object?

Further, he would never be able to show it to anyone for fear of being caught. Everyone at school had seen the key and knew it was Ms. Brock's. It had no real purpose to Lucas. As far as he knew, he was merely fascinated by its appearance. Yet he felt a strange, esoteric attachment to it and couldn't, for the life of him, part with it.

2

RETURNING THE KEY

As the school day progressed, the hallways buzzed with chatter about the mysterious disappearance of the key.

Everyone wondered aloud, "What could have happened to it?"

Theories began circulating, ranging from the belief that the key possessed magical qualities, had vanished and would re-emerge on its own, to speculation about it being stolen by a pickpocket from Ms. Brock's purse. Others assumed it was misplaced somewhere in the school, which resulted in organized searches over lunch break to find it.

Unbeknownst to all, the key remained nestled in Lucas's pocket. He was not able to concentrate on anything else. In fact, when asked a question in history class, a subject he knew well, he just stuttered and acted as though he did not understand the question. Sensing his distraction, his teacher moved on to another student, figuring he was just having a difficult day.

In the meantime, Ms. Brock retraced the steps of her visit to Diyton South Side, trying to piece together every move made to identify where the key could be. It had no significant monetary value, but it had served as a meaningful icon to the Sharefield Central High School theater program for the past two years. She had hopes of making it a school tradition by using it in all future performances.

After school, Lucas attended his private guitar lesson with an accomplished musician in the area. He was learning quickly. Lucas had grown very fond of music by listening to the old tunes his parents played on their record player. There was always music in the house, and he knew the words to many past hits. Wanting to create music of his own, he had begun experimenting with a used guitar he received last winter. These private lessons helped him to master the mechanics of playing the instrument, along with acquiring a better understanding of music theory.

Following his lesson that day, Lucas got an interesting idea. The well-equipped Diyton hardware store had just about anything one would need, from tools, paint, repair kits, and various other home supplies. Lucas decided to try to make a duplicate key so he could return the original to Ms. Brock while keeping one for himself.

He headed down to the store, the same one that Dion had visited in his virtual world experience earlier that year. There, he encountered George, the store's most knowledgeable employee for home repair jobs. Lucas showed him the key and asked if there was any way to make a copy of it.

George said, "You're in luck. We have recently installed a computerized key reproduction machine. It scans keys, performs the necessary calculations, and then drives a cutter to reproduce not only the key's mechanical code but also any decorative highlights on the key face. Let's check the machine to see if it supports the exact shape of your key."

The two of them walked over to the futuristic-looking key reproduction machine. It was about the size of a vending machine but far more complicated. The device boasted a display panel with a touch screen that showed all sorts of scanning and cutting options. George proceeded to scroll through the key shape options on the display, looking for an exact match to the one Lucas was holding.

"There it is," said Lucas. He pointed to the screen as the blank key shape scrolled by.

"Good eye," George nodded in appreciation.

The image did not show any detail of the key, just the outline. According to the instructions on the display, the user was to insert their key into the slot at the top of the machine before pressing the START button.

"That sounds easy enough," said Lucas, pushing the key headfirst into the open slot. The machine came alive, droning and whirring with motor sounds as it scanned the key from all directions. A bright light emanated from along the seams of the machine where the outside enclosure pieces came together.

After a minute or so, the key machine went silent.

Lucas asked, "Is it finished?"

"Not quite," said George.

Then, a loud grinding sound came rumbling out of the machine, indicating that it was cutting a key to match the scanned image. This continued for another couple of minutes. Lucas finally heard a brass key drop behind the door of an opening near the bottom of the machine, like a penny clanging onto a metal floor. George retrieved the shiny new key and handed it to Lucas, who examined it carefully. It was a perfect match of the original. A huge grin spread across his face until he turned the key over.

The back side of the key had a distinctively unique design on it. Perplexed, Lucas showed the key to George, who shared his surprise. "I have no idea. This has never happened before. Strange…" He handed the key back to Lucas.

Lucas thought, *This is fantastic.*

He couldn't help but feel thrilled by the unexpected twist. To him, the new key was so much better than the original. In his mind, it was a one-of-a-kind magical artifact.

"How do we get the original key back?" he asked George.

"Well, it is supposed to eject on its own after the reproduction. For some reason, it has not."

Lucas was starting to panic. "We must get it back! It does not belong to me."

George looked at Lucas funny. "What do you mean?"

"It's okay," said Lucas in an attempt to be reassuring, "I found it and plan to return it to its owner."

"Then what are you doing with its copy?" George narrowed his eyes.

"It's not what you think. The key does not open a lock, at least as far as I know. It is just a prop used in theater productions."

George was not satisfied with the answer, but decided to drop the matter for now. It was none of his business unless there was real criminal intent. Lucas did not look like a crook to him. Still, he was a bit suspicious.

Lucas repeated his question, "How can we recover the original key?"

George flipped a latch on the side of the machine that opened it up. Lucas was impressed with the complex mechanisms inside. The original key was stuck behind the input slot in a clamp, which George released by hand, and the key was freed. He handed it to Lucas, who thanked him and put it in his pocket with the updated version they had just made. He paid for the reproduction and then headed back home.

On the way home, he studied the new key and marveled at its two different faces. The following day, he took the original key to the central office and put it on the desk early in the morning before the staff arrived. It was discovered as soon as the school administrator showed up that morning.

The principal proclaimed the key's recovery during morning announcements. She suggested that whoever turned it in identify themselves, but no one came forward.

That same morning, the principal of Diyton South Side called Ms. Brock to inform her that the key had been found. Ms. Brock was elated. She planned to retrieve it that very evening after school. She was relieved to have her key back in her possession for future theater performances. Ms. Brock told everyone at Sharefield Central how it just showed up on the administrator's desk at the other school.

The Sharefield Gang visited her later that evening to see the key and reminisce about their past performances in which the key had played a major part.

Little did Ms. Brock know of the profound impact the key had on the gang's adventures outside of the classroom, away from theater, in their real world. These included both the game they experienced on the old *Commodore 64* computer and the imaginary world of *The Lost View* they had created with the help of the AI-equipped glasses they had gotten from Chelsea's father.

3

THE TWO BOYS MEET

As summer approached, Lucas prepared to try out for a select soccer team based in Sharefield, just ten miles away. His parents fully supported the program and ensured that he was able to attend all the practices and games.

Lucas got word from friends at school that some of the boys planning to try out for the team were practicing at Sharefield Park on Saturday mornings. He asked his mom to take him there for a scrimmage game just two weeks before tryouts were scheduled to start. She happily obliged.

Upon arrival at the park, Lucas could hear music in the background. He was drawn to the melodic sounds of a band

rehearsing nearby. The band featured a couple of guitar players and several handheld percussion musicians, all playing
along with a small brass section. They sounded crisp and
well-rehearsed, harmonizing in perfect time to familiar songs
of the day. A sign beside the band said that they would be
performing at a Sharefield festival later in the summer. After
enjoying the music for a few minutes, Lucas headed over to
the soccer field.

He spotted Nate that morning, one of the best players
in town. Once enough players gathered, they split into two
teams for a scrimmage match. Nate was appointed captain
of one team, while a boy named Jake captained the other
team. They were to flip a coin to decide which team would
start from the west goal, which was facing the piercing mid-
morning sun in their eyes. It was a clear disadvantage to play
from that direction.

Nate said, "Does anyone have a coin?"

The boys were all dressed to play soccer; no one had put a
coin in their short pockets.

Lucas recalled his special key, which he always carried with
him. He considered it his good luck charm. He thought to
himself, *Well, I have a two-sided key, but I am not so sure that
I want to show it here.* But reflexively then, he simply reached
into his pocket and suggested using it. "I have a key here that
has two different sides. Perhaps we can toss it in place of a
coin," he said sheepishly with all eyes on him.

He handed the key to Nate, who took one look at it and
felt chills up and down his spine. He did not want to make a

scene in front of everyone, so skipping over any drama on the soccer field, he regained his composure and announced, "The side with the leaf is tails. Jake, you call it in the air."

He flipped the key off his thumb as he would a coin. The key spun around high into the air, flickering like a star in the night as the sun caught its face with each revolution.

Lucas could still hear the music in the background and recognized the tune. He said quietly to himself, although others, including Nate, who was standing next to him, could hear him say, "The key of C." Lucas was referring to the music, but the others did not interpret it that way.

Right then, the sun hit the key at just the perfect angle so that it quite momentarily reflected the letter 'C' prominently onto Jake's jersey just as he called out, "Tails!"

Lucas and the others all saw the flash of light on Jake's jersey. The key hit the ground and bounced once, then landed with the leaf side up.

Nate looked at the key and proclaimed, "It's tails. You win the toss. Which side of the field do you want?"

Jake immediately replied, "We will take the east side." The obvious choice.

Nate picked up the key and examined it for a few seconds. He noticed that there was a 'C' on its face around the leaf, then returned it to Lucas. Nate looked straight at him, probing for a connection, but Lucas stared back with a blank look. Nate wanted to say something but realized that now was not the time for conversation.

With everyone eager to start playing, the focus shifted back to soccer. The game began shortly.

As Jake's team took to the field, Lucas remarked to him, "Did you notice the reflection of the letter 'C' on your jersey as the key flew through the air?"

Jake replied jokingly, "That's strange. I was watching the key glistening in the sun, not my own jersey. I did hear you say, 'the key of C.' Maybe you have special powers we can use on the soccer field." They shared a laugh.

"Well," said Lucas, "there really was a clear 'C' on your jersey for just a moment as the key went flying."

Jake shrugged his shoulders and replied, "Stranger things have happened."

Lucas began to realize that this key was more than just a beautiful good-luck charm.

Having not played much soccer since moving to Diyton, Lucas found himself surprised at the park in Sharefield. The boys, all about the same age, some being as big and strong as he was, played with intensity. With no referees or timekeepers in the informal scrimmage, the game was fast and rough.

Players were knocking each other to the ground at every opportunity. Nate and Lucas stood out, dominating the opposing teams. No one really kept the score, although both sides scored several goals. The scrimmage became more of a challenge between players to show who was the best. The select team tryouts were just two weeks away.

At one point, when the boys took a break, Nate remarked, "We're spending more time on the ground than kicking the ball."

As play resumed, two players on Nate's team collided with Lucas, simultaneously sending him straight to the ground on his side. It was clearly an accident. He felt the key in his pocket digging into his thigh, along with a jarring sensation in his head. It seemed as though there was a strange resonance set up between the motion in his head and the key in his pocket. He lay still on the field for what seemed like hours, although, in actuality, only a minute or so. Everyone gathered around as Lucas slowly shook his head and came back to the present moment. He felt fine and announced, "I'm alright." Getting up on his feet, Lucas walked around to regain his composure. His peers observed him for any signs of injury, but he seemed healthy. Lucas yelled out, "Come on, let's resume play."

Nate suggested calling it a day, noting the late hour. Lucas checked his watch and agreed.

"You are right. The morning sure went by fast. My mom will be here to pick me up in less than ten minutes." Everyone decided to end the scrimmage. Nate was agonizing over how to approach Lucas, but his mother arrived early. He jumped in the car before Nate could figure out the right words.

That evening, plenty of sore muscles and bruises plagued the players from the highly physical game. Lucas did not think much of his fall, casually mentioning it to his parents as dinner conversation. His dad suggested a hospital check-up, just as a precaution. So, they headed to the Sharefield General Hospital right away. Diyton had a couple of hospitals of its own, but Sharefield's emergency trauma care team had a reputation that was second to none.

It was late evening when the hospital staff began running some tests on Lucas. They then decided it would be best for him to spend the night for observation while awaiting the test results.

During the night, Lucas had a peculiarly fantastical dream that felt so alarmingly real that he woke up thinking that he was actually living it. He dreamt that the hospital was using an incredibly old personal computer called the *Commodore 64* to analyze his test and was drawing incorrect conclusions from the results. Upon waking up in the morning, he remembered the hospital staff combing through a stack of books in his dream, along with the old computer, trying to understand the test results and assessing how to treat his injury.

This was all quite unsettling to Lucas. He felt much better when a smiling nurse came in to greet him.

She said in a soothing voice, "You had been talking in your sleep all night long." She handed him a menu and asked him what he would like for breakfast. Lucas, feeling hungry, responded, "I'll take two of everything," eliciting laughter from both.

"Will that be two eggs, over easy?" asked the nurse.

"How about two eggs over and over again," said Lucas.

With a slight grin, the nurse replied, "I will have them add an extra piece of toast."

After the nurse left, Lucas rummaged through his clothes and recovered the key from his pants pocket. He pulled it out and looked at it. It had become a source of comfort to him.

The sun streamed through the large window of his fifth-floor room, casting a beam of light onto the key. As Lucas examined it, he could see what looked like a stack of books in the center part of the key. *That is strange*, he thought. *I must be hallucinating.* Flipping it over, he was stunned to see the image of the very hospital where he was staying on the reverse side.

This is impossible, he thought. Turning the key back, Lucas once again saw the medical textbooks. As he flipped the key over a second time, there it unmistakably was: the Sharefield General Hospital.

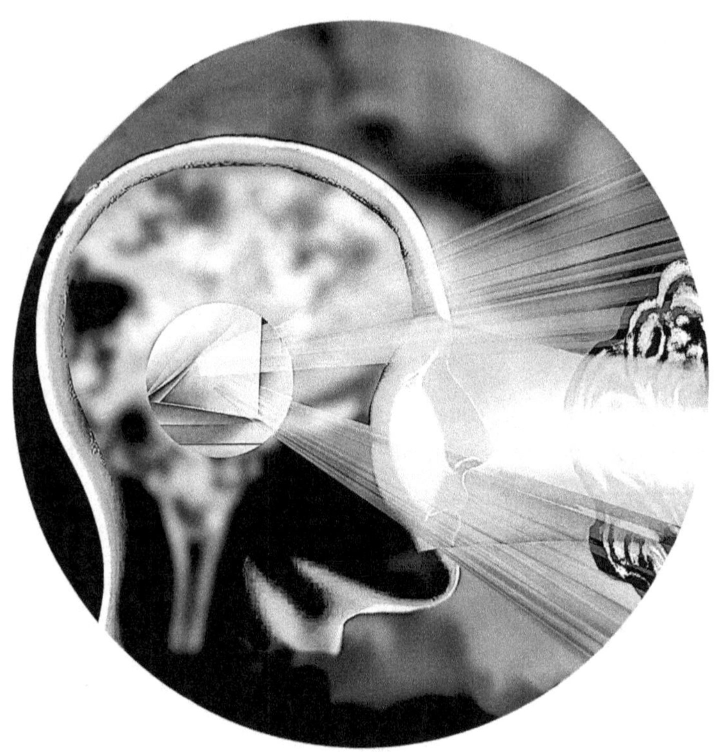

REFLECTION

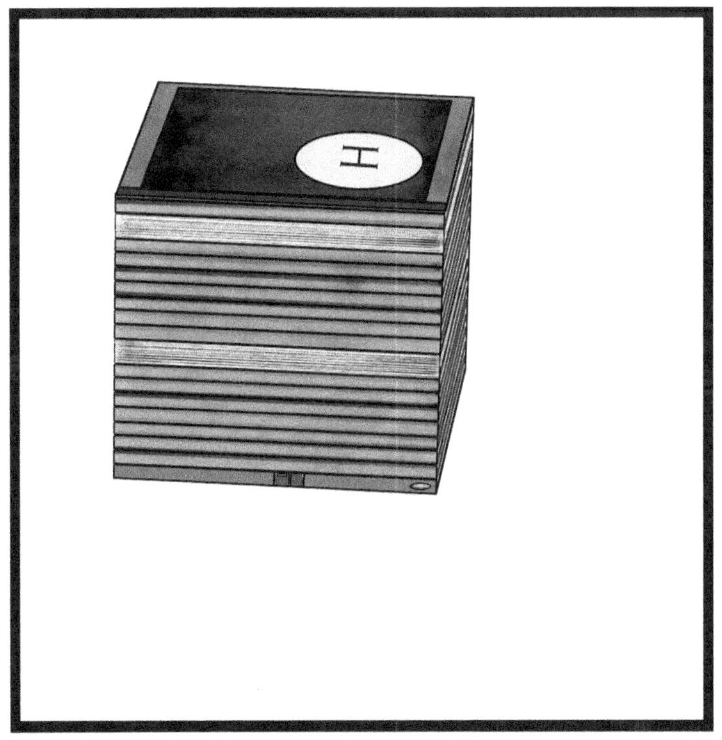

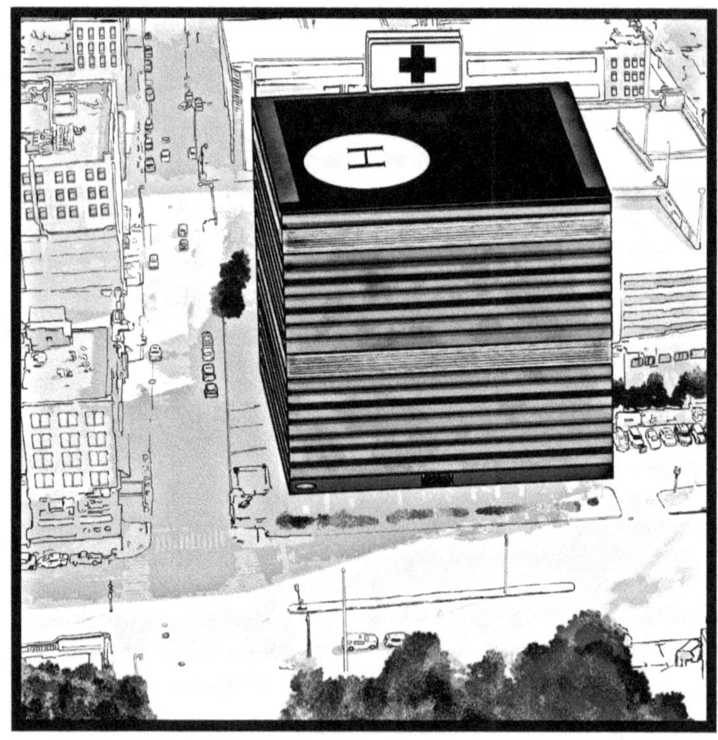

He tucked the key back into his pocket, unsure of what to make of his condition. *Maybe there is something seriously wrong with me*, he mused.

Just then, a doctor entered his room. He said, "I have good news. You appear to have no serious injuries. All your tests were negative. We plan to release you from the hospital this morning."

Soon after, his parents arrived, already aware of the good news. They sat with Lucas as he enjoyed a hearty breakfast before preparing for his discharge.

During their drive back to Diyton, Lucas recounted his strange dream to his parents. They found it quite amusing. His dad said, "It is going to take more than an old home computer to figure out some of the nutty things you do, like refusing to tie your shoestrings most of the time."

"I like to save on shoestring wear and tear," Lucas replied with a smile.

He chose not to mention the odd images he saw in the key. Once home, he went straight to his room and once again pulled the key from his pocket. Upon scrutinizing it, he could not see anything special in it anymore. There were no strange images in the center of the key; nothing. He wondered if perhaps the lighting in the hospital had something to do with it, so he walked over to his bedroom window and held the key up in the sunlight. Still he found no images in the key. He began to think that he had imagined the whole thing. After all, he had been through quite an ordeal over the past day. It was his first stay in a hospital.

As the day wore on, he couldn't stop thinking about what he had seen in the key that morning. He made it a point to check the key often for images despite finding nothing each time.

Deep down, Lucas knew he had something incredibly special in his possession.

4

THIS KEY IS SPECIAL

The following week of classes proved exceptionally challenging as the end-of-year tests were rapidly approaching. The students from both Diyton South Side and Sharefield Central worked diligently to finish the school year in the best of standing.

Lucas was looking forward to the weekend and the soccer scrimmage on Saturday morning at Sharefield Park. It would be the last practice before the select team tryouts the following weekend. Feeling strong and prepared, Lucas looked forward to giving his best effort during the scrimmage.

Meanwhile, Nate had been wondering how Lucas, the new boy from Diyton, was doing after his fall last Saturday. He sensed that Lucas would soon become a significant part of his life and the lives of the rest of the gang. After all, he had a key that partially matched the ones that Nate and the Sharefield Gang had come to know very well through their adventures over the past year. That week at school Nate had shared with the rest of the gang about his brief encounter with Lucas and the key of the same shape with two different sides. A side they were familiar with and another one they had seen only briefly in a strange world of virtual reality.

The gang decided to attend the next Saturday morning's scrimmage in hopes of meeting Lucas in person.

As Lucas's father dropped him off that morning, he mentioned he needed to run some errands and wouldn't be back for several hours. That suited Lucas just fine. He was ready for a full scrimmage of soccer that morning. *Besides*, he thought to himself, *there are other things going on at Sharefield Park on Saturday mornings.*

This included the band rehearsal he heard and enjoyed last week. With the special key in his pocket, he looked forward to the day ahead. The key had not shown him any more images since the previous weekend, yet Lucas still couldn't shake the feeling that it possessed powers that were beyond his comprehension.

Nate, rushing to make it to the scrimmage on time, grabbed a bran muffin and his water bottle from his mother. Bran muffins were his favorite, and his mother insisted he eat something before all the exercise. Nate enjoyed his snack as he made his way to the park, inadvertently leaving a few crumbs behind for the birds.

Arriving just in time, Nate spotted Lucas and approached him to ask if he felt okay after last Saturday's fall. Lucas informed him that he ended up spending a night in the hospital but that he felt okay afterward. "The tests they ran showed that there was no injury."

Nate replied, "I am awfully glad to hear that. You know, several of my friends are going to watch the scrimmage this morning. Would you like to meet them and get acquainted after our match?"

Lucas agreed. In fact, he was thrilled at the opportunity to meet Nate's friends. Nate was one of the best players on the field and Lucas figured they would be teammates over the summer season. Being new in the area, Lucas was always looking to make new friends.

As the players selected sides for the match, the other members of the Sharefield Gang settled in along the sidelines to watch. The teams ended up being quite similar to those who played against each other last weekend. This time, one of the players had brought a coin for the toss.

The scrimmage was as exhilarating as any sanctioned match, with outstanding, almost heroic individual performances along with good coordination between the players and unselfish teamwork. This week's practice session was different than last, perhaps because the coach was there to watch. Although the score wasn't officially kept, both goalies faced numerous challenging shots throughout the match. After the scrimmage, Nate and Lucas walked to the sidelines together. Nate asked, "Did you notice that the coach was writing in a notebook the entire scrimmage session?" Lucas replied, "He must have been analyzing our every move."

"Yes," said Nate with a grin, "he's making a list and checking it twice."

The boys regrouped with the rest of the Sharefield Gang. After short introductions, they headed to their favorite spot in the park, under a giant oak tree. It was the same tree where they had discussed their trip up Majestic Mountain the summer before. It was here where they had first seen images through their virtual reality glasses. The gang had some history with this tree, all right. They all felt a sense of anticipation, as if something significant was going to happen once again. Another turning point in their lives was on the horizon.

Nate kicked the conversation off by praising his fellow soccer player for his impressive performance and his amazing athletic abilities. Lucas, feeling humbled, reciprocated the compliments to Nate. The two boys shared a mutual respect for each other's abilities and their love of the game.

Kim then took the lead and said, "Nate tells us that you have a special key that was used in last week's scrimmage for the coin toss."

"Yes, I do," said Lucas. "And the more I think about it, I am beginning to believe that it has special powers."

"Really," said Kim. "Perhaps you are not alone." Lucas stared back, confused.

"Can we see the key?" asked Chelsea.

Lucas said, "I don't normally show it around, but I always keep it in my pocket." With that, he pulled out the key for everyone to see.

The gang was on their feet, agitated, moving around, curious to have a look. They knew more about the key and its significance than Lucas himself. He handed the key to Chelsea, who looked at both its sides and proclaimed, "The back side matches the image of the key we saw in our final virtual reality session from the world of The Lost View."

Kim said, "Let me see," and recognizing both sides of the key confirmed, saying, "Yes, and the front side is just like the one in our school play this year and last."

Lucas replied, "Well, I can explain that." He told the story of finding Ms. Brock's key and making a copy at the Diyton Hardware store.

"That is interesting," said Dion. He also observed the key closely before passing it along for everyone else to inspect.

The last one to examine it was Nate. As he held it, he started to laugh.

"What is so funny?" asked Anthony.

"I don't know," said Nate, it is just that I have never seen a key like this before." As he handed the key back to Lucas,

Lucas noticed something strange. It suddenly looked different to him. He did not understand what was happening.

He said out loud for everyone to hear, "You know, all of a sudden, I see something different in this key. It's an image of a bran muffin reflecting off the center!" He was absolutely convinced of what he saw. On the key's flip side, the image of a muffin became a pencil eraser, again at the center of the key.

"What in the world just happened?" He exclaimed, "Now it's a pencil eraser."

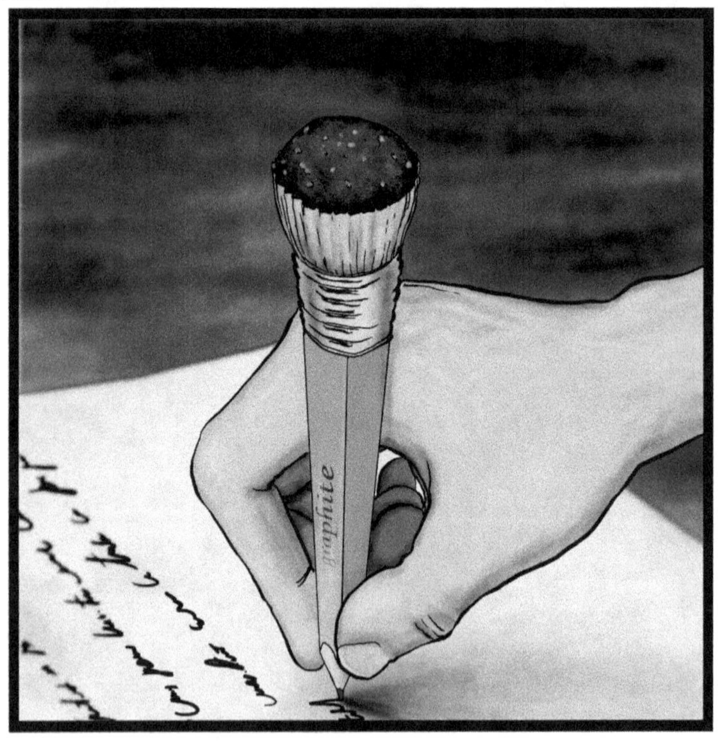
graphite

Nate said, "You see what?"

Lucas held the key up for everyone to see, but the others saw the same two-sided key they had each examined a minute ago.

Perplexed, Lucas observed it again, and indeed it was the same as before." The gang was starting to wonder if Lucas was alright.

He repeated, "The images are gone. I don't see them anymore."

"You're probably imagining it," said Anthony, before taking the key from Lucas.

Anthony examined both sides again and proclaimed, "Looks like a double-sided key to me; no breakfast in here writing graphite graffiti."

Everyone chuckled as he handed the key back to Lucas. He replied, "Well, it was different for me. I definitely saw a muffin in the middle of this key. I wonder what the significance could be."

Nate replied, "I did have a bran muffin for breakfast this morning. I might have mentioned it during the scrimmage; my stomach was a little upset." The group thought that was rather funny, but no one wanted to laugh aloud.

To change the subject, Lucia said, "I wish we had a nice bakery here in Sharefield."

"Yes, but we do have an exquisite restaurant, The Pony Pizza," replied Anthony.

Lucia interjected, "You mean the Mustang Pizzeria."

"Victor liked that restaurant, too," Kim added.

"Who is Victor?" asked Lucas.

"He is our friend. He moved to the coast near the beginning of the school year," explained Nate. "We miss him. He is close to the ocean and enjoys all that it has to offer. He shares his many wonderful new experiences out there with us."

"We all stay in touch with him. I think he misses us as well. He grew up here and was always a part of the Sharefield Gang," Kim elaborated.

"Speaking of which," said Dion, "Lucas, we have a connection with you beyond what you might know. You're one of us."

Surprised, Lucas asked, "What do you mean?"

"We'll get to that," Chelsea intervened. "It's all connected to your key." Chelsea was instantly attracted to Lucas's smile and calm demeanor. She really wanted to get to know him better. Fortunately, she was sure that she would have the chance.

Lucas spoke up, "Let me tell you about the dream I had in the hospital." Lucas proceeded to recount the story of the books that the medical staff used to diagnose him, along with the antique Commodore 64 computer. He explained how an image of a stack of books appeared in the key that morning before transforming on the back side of the key into an image of the same hospital in which he was staying.

"That's more than weird, that's outrageous," exclaimed Dion. He told Lucas about the antiquated Commodore 64 computer that they had found in the old man's mansion.

Intrigued, Lucas asked about the computer. "It's still around, but it no longer works," was Dion's reply.

Lucas shared, "I am interested in computers as well. Perhaps we can look at it sometime."

"That might turn out to be insightful," said Dion.

Lucia interjected and said, "This is all just too unbelievable."

Kim, adopting a stern tone, said, "Lucas, we know who you are."

"What?" he said.

Kim asked him, "Was your grandfather's name Fred?"

"Well, yes, it was. He was a star football player. You must have guessed because you've heard of him, and of course, we share the same last name."

"No," Chelsea clarified, "most of us don't know a lot about football, but we knew your grandfather. We used to visit him at the Sharefield Assisted Living Facility."

"Really, you knew my grandfather?" Lucas asked, surprised. "I don't remember much about him. I had not seen him since I was a young boy. We moved out of state when my parents were transferred away from this area. We only recently returned to Diyton. I knew my grandfather's death had an impact on my dad, who thought differently after the funeral. We stayed in a couple rooms in an old mansion up on a hill here in town that was converted into a bed and breakfast."

"Was the place clean?" said Anthony with a half-grin.

"It was well kept," said Lucas. He continued, "So how did you know for sure that I was Fred's grandson if it wasn't the rather common name?

"It's a long story," said Kim. She and Lucia proceeded to fill Lucas in on all the events that took place in their virtual world of The Lost View. Lucas listened intently, looking spellbound. She also spoke of Victor.

Anthony interjected, saying, "Victor is always thinking of others. He made sure we had special delicious things to eat on our journey up Majestic Mountain. The brownies his mother made for us at his request were exceptional. He knew we all love chocolate."

"So where does that leave us now?" Lucas questioned. "Why does this key have two different sides? Why am I seeing images in it that no one else can see? How are these images transforming as I turn the key over? What messages are they sending us?"

No one had answers, but one thing was certain: the key was special. It needed to be protected and kept secret.

Kim proposed, "Lucas has a magical key that we cannot explain. We must all agree right here to keep it to ourselves until we can figure out more about it. Is everyone in agreement?"

The circle of friends all nodded their heads as Lucas affirmed, "I will not reveal the secrets of the key outside of this gang until the appropriate time."

5

SOCCER TRYOUTS

The official Sharefield select soccer team tryouts were scheduled for the following Saturday morning. Lucas spent every evening of the week before the tryouts practicing with a few friends at a local field. He always kept the key in his pocket and checked it occasionally, just to make sure it was still there and to see if it showed him anything new.

The Sharefield Gang was immersed in studying for their end-of-year tests. Lucia, who was an all-around good student, began pondering what profession she might like to pursue as an adult. She had always been interested in clothing design and received numerous accolades for her costume work in Sharefield theater productions, over the past two years. She realized this was not something she needed to contemplate right away. Although aware of this, the thought lingered as she studied for the tests.

She thoroughly enjoyed designing clothing and felt like it was in her blood. Doing anything else seemed hard for her to imagine. Yet, her parents reminded her of the big world of opportunities beyond design. For some reason, the weight of the decision burdened her this week, maybe because she was juggling multiple subjects for exams. She spoke about clothing design often and had even brought it up during last Saturday's discussion under the big oak tree in Sharefield Park.

The week rolled around quickly. Soon it was Friday night before the soccer tryouts. Lucas and Nate both had gone to bed early. Before drifting off to sleep, Lucas placed the key on his nightstand as he did most evenings, often with a sense of trepidation, because he never knew what he might see in it. To his surprise, a new image appeared on the key - a picture of a chocolate kiss. He immediately turned the key over and found the kiss transformed into the sail of a beautiful yacht on the water.

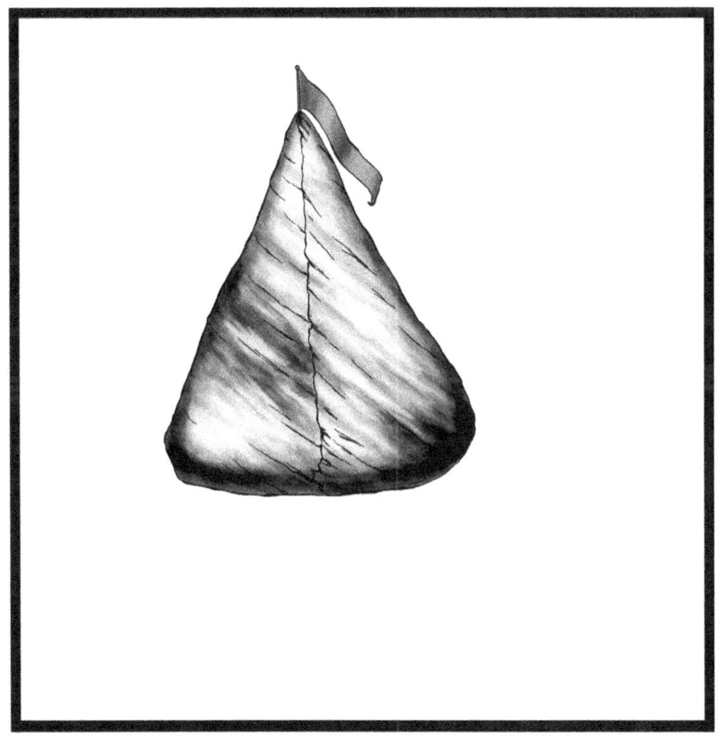

Intrigued yet unsettled, Lucas spent much of the night thinking about the significance of these images. He had not seen any images in the key over the past week and thought there would be no more, but it was happening again. He wondered, *Why do I keep seeing these things?* It made going to sleep arduous. He tried making connections between a chocolate kiss in his key and a sailboat before falling asleep. Chelsea, Lucia, and Kim decided to go to the park Saturday morning to watch the soccer action and catch up with Lucas and Nate after the tryouts.

Everyone arrived at the field at about the same time that morning, a few minutes before the tryouts were to start. The ensemble that had been in the park for the past several weeks was already practicing. At Lucas's suggestion, the gang settled on the grass to listen to them. Lucas felt that the music would help him and his new friend Nate relax, before the tryouts began.

As they sat there enjoying the music, Lucas took out the remarkable key. He was hoping there would be no distraction from it so that he could concentrate on soccer. So, to ease his sheer curiosity he looked at the key before the tryouts started. Unfortunately, but no longer as a surprise, a new image could be seen in the key. The chocolate kiss and the sailboat were gone. This time he saw what looked like a sewing thimble. Lucas turned the key over and watched the thimble transform into the lampshade of a living room lamp.

He showed it to the girls, but they saw the same key they had seen before. When they handed the key back to Lucas, the images had vanished for him as well.

Even though the others could not see anything in the key and were skeptical about its special powers, they listened intently to Lucas's description of the key's image transformation. Lucia immediately recognized the significance of the imagery.

She said, "I've been contemplating sewing and clothing design all week. This apparent sign has just shined a light on it for me. I'm now more inclined than ever to pursue a career in clothing design.

Just then, the shrill of a loud whistle pierced their ears. Nate and Lucas knew what that meant. They both sprang into action, racing to the soccer field where they joined the rest of the players for ball-handling drills. Coach Newman, familiar with most of the boys since he scouted them, including Lucas and Nate, observed their performance closely. After a series of challenging drills to showcase agility and ball control, the coach divided the players into two teams.

Coach Newman assigned positions to each player, designating both Nate and Lucas as Strikers. They were two of the most dominant players on the field. Their mission was to receive passes and put the ball into the back of the net by out-maneuvering defenders through technical prowess and speed. The scrimmage captivated the girls and other spectators, with every player giving it their all. Each of them wanted to impress the coach for a spot on the summer select team.

Becoming a part of this team meant opportunities to travel to new places and play teams from various cities and towns. The intense scrimmage lasted well over two hours, leaving the boys exhausted.

Coach Newman said that he would post the roster of players who made the cut on the website he had set up for the team. The boys could check the site sometime the following Monday for status updates. He thanked the boys for their dedication to the sport and mentioned that he would carefully consider each and every player. Still, only so many players could be on the roster.

The potential team members headed home, their muscles sore but spirits lifted by the prospect of making the team.

That same afternoon, Anthony received a lengthy message from Victor. He had gotten a chance to go sailing on a beautiful yacht that belonged to his friend's father. Victor described the thrill of working as part of the crew and mastering the art of trimming sails based on wind, the direction of the boat and sailing conditions. "Being on that magnificent boat was an exhilarating experience as it almost flew through the water, effortlessly bouncing through waves, driven by the powerful forces of the wind," he told Anthony.He also confided in Anthony about feeling particularly homesick and missing the Sharefield Gang. The two exchanged texts for a good half-hour. Victor even sent a picture of the boat and the crew. Afterward, Anthony reached out to Kim and informed her about Victor's homesickness.

Kim replied, "That's strange. The key predicted this. I know just what to do. Victor loves chocolate. I will package up some chocolate kisses and send them to him."

"I think that was the message in the key," Kim explained to Anthony, referencing what Lucas had seen that morning.

Anthony pondered, "Is it really the key, or is Lucas the one seeing all these images?"

"That's a good question," Kim responded. "Maybe it's a combination. Lucas seems to be the only one who can see things in the key, but we've known such keys to hold mystical powers in our past."

Anthony added, "Indeed, it's uncanny how he ended up with a key that has two different sides in the first place."

As Monday morning arrived, the boys who had tried out for the Sharefield select soccer team eagerly checked the website to see who had made the team. There were no postings early morning before school, so the boys would have to wait until lunch to check again. Nate, particularly anxious, visited the soccer website as soon as his last morning classes ended but still found no results.

The coach is really taking his time, Nate thought to himself. *It must be difficult for him. There were a lot of exceptionally capable players out there on Saturday. This would be an arduous task for anyone.*

He checked his phone for results one last time after lunch break, but to no avail. His afternoon classes seemed to last forever as he waited anxiously to check the roster. After his last class, he bumped into Jake, who somberly informed him that he didn't make the team. In a low voice, he said, "I am sorry you will not be a part of the team this summer. You should have made the cut." Nate looked stunned. He wasn't sure about being the absolute best player on the field, but he felt he was certainly one of the top players in Sharefield.

Still in a state of shock, Nate pulled out his phone and checked the team website for himself. He noted that the coach had posted the team just a few minutes prior. As his eyes scanned down the list of names like a speed-reader in a timed contest, he instantaneously recognized and agreed with most of the choices the coach had made. As he ran across Lucas's name, he smiled. Abruptly, he reached the bottom of the list without finding his own name, and a wave of devastation washed over him.

How could this be? he thought, *What am I going to do now?* As he walked home, he tried to calm himself down and accept the situation, but inside, he felt utterly crushed.

As soon as he arrived home, Nate drafted an email to coach Newman expressing his disappointment but also that he accepted the decision. He promised to work even harder to earn a spot on the team next year. Accepting defeat wasn't easy for Nate, especially after putting in so much effort for the tryouts. He felt he had performed well at the tryout session, but evidently, the coach disagreed.

About an hour later, he received a call from an unknown number. Still distraught, Nate answered it in a somber voice. It turned out to be Coach Newman. He explained that he had made a mistake. A week ago, he had listed everyone who had signed up for tryouts in his notepad. A couple of the players did not make it to the tryout session. "Perhaps they changed their mind," explained Coach Newman. He had erased their names at the tryout session before transferring the list to the computer that evening. The coach explained to Nate that he had inadvertently erased his name instead of the one above it. Although he apologized for the mistake and expressed the desire to have Nate on the team, he couldn't undo the posted roster of twenty players. The roster would have to stand unless one of the players decided not to join the squad.

Nate was beside himself. He wanted to play on the team so badly. He thanked Coach Newman for the call and hung up, wondering just how he would manage to watch the others play in a league he knew he deserved to be a part of.

He was almost silent at dinner that evening. As he studied for his upcoming end-of-year test, his phone rang once again. This time, he recognized Coach Newman's number. He answered it with an anticipatory voice, "Hello, hello," he said.

Coach Newman said, "Nate, we have an open slot for you on the team. One of the players has decided to play with a different organization, so I would like to officially invite you to join the Sharefield Select Team for the summer league."

Ecstatic, Nate thanked Coach Newman profusely before ending the call with a huge grin on his face and determination in his heart. He reaffirmed to himself, *I am going to play on the select soccer team this summer!*

Then he remembered the vision in the key that Lucas had seen before the tryouts. A bran muffin that became a pencil eraser. The key had shown Lucas an image related to his Saturday morning tryout and predicted the coach's mistake with the roster. *This is really strange*, he thought to himself. *We have got to understand more about that key and how Lucas sees visions in it. For the moment, I want to celebrate by sharing the good news with the gang.*

He decided to call Lucas first, who was delighted to hear from him. Lucas said, "I thought there just had to be a mistake. You are an awesome soccer player."

Nate replied, "Thank you, my friend, so are you. We'll have a fantastic time playing together this summer."

"That's for sure," said Nate.

Before Nate hung up the phone, he reminded Lucas about the bran muffin that became a pencil eraser.

Lucas replied, "This is happening more and more. I don't know what to make of it." Nate said, "Neither do I, but it sure is mysterious. Anyway, see you at soccer practice next week."

The two boys hung up, both pondering what the key might reveal next.

6

THE ORIGIN OF KEYS

Monday after school was the first day of practice for the soccer team. Nate and Lucas were both thrilled to be a part of it. Coach Newman's opening speech emphasized the importance of unity, fostering quick bonding among the players.

After practice, Lucas approached Nate and said, "These key images are really getting to me. We need to figure out what's going on. Do you have any ideas?" Nate was still not a hundred percent convinced that the key alone was responsible for all the strange images. This was especially true since everything Lucas saw was relevant to his daily life and that of his friends.

Only he saw the visions in that key. However, Nate thought, *"Knowing what I do about the magic of keys from my past, maybe this key does have special powers."*

So, he suggested to Lucas, "Let's dig in and investigate this together."

That evening, Nate called Kim to share the events of the day and the peculiar vision of the bran muffin that turned into a pencil eraser. Kim, already aware of the soccer roster mix-up, proposed that the Sharefield Gang meet at her house after school the following day to brainstorm possible ways to unravel the mystery of Lucas's double-sided key.

At school the next day, Kim asked the gang to convene at her house after classes. She gave Lucas a call and included him. She made a point of asking him to bring his key along. She also suggested that Dion bring the old key he had found behind the waterfalls during last year's class picnic. Dion agreed, saying, "yes, it might be useful."

When everyone gathered at Kim's house, Dion shared with Lucas his key's story, telling of its resemblance to the one used in their school plays. He had also brought the old Commodore 64 computer with him, even though it did not work, just in case it might add something to the conversation. Dion pulled out his key and passed it around.

The gang reminisced about the adventures surrounding that key and the relevance of one that looked just like it in their virtual world of *The Lost View*. Intrigued, Lucas absorbed their stories, now firmly convinced of the key's extraordinary nature. He was eager to work with the others to understand the strange occurrences associated with the two-sided key.

Kim interjected, "Ms. Brock is quite fond of her key and keeps it in her desk in the theater room. She talks about finding a way to incorporate it into next year's play."

She then turned to Lucas and said, "Let's start by revisiting, once again, how you found that key in the first place."

"As you know, it's a bit of a long story," said Lucas. "Before I begin, I must tell you I have seen yet another pair of images in my key. I was holding the key in my hand while speaking with Kim on the phone earlier today, and I saw a padlock on one side of the key. I turned it over, and the lock became a purse in a lady's arms. This is strange because the story of my key begins with a lady and her purse. Ms. Brock, to be more precise."

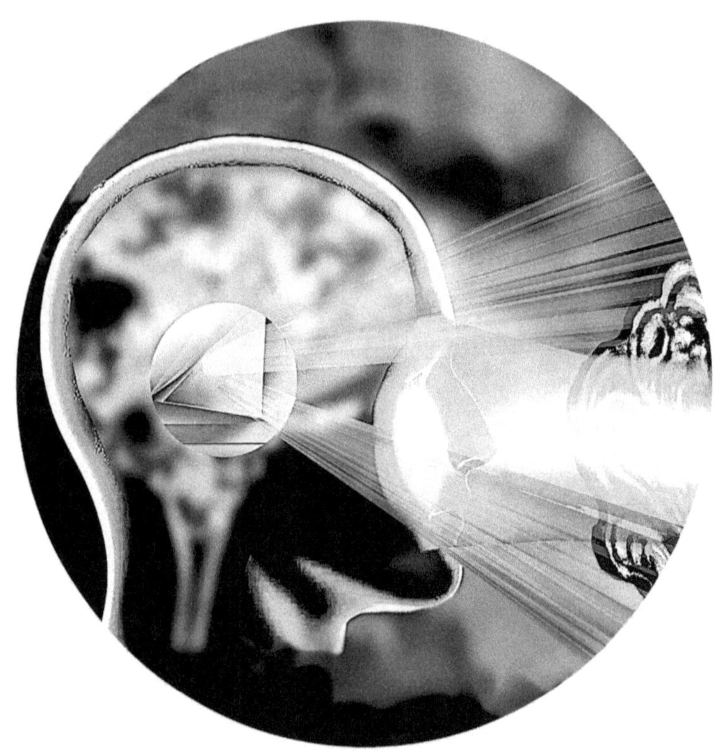

REFLECTION

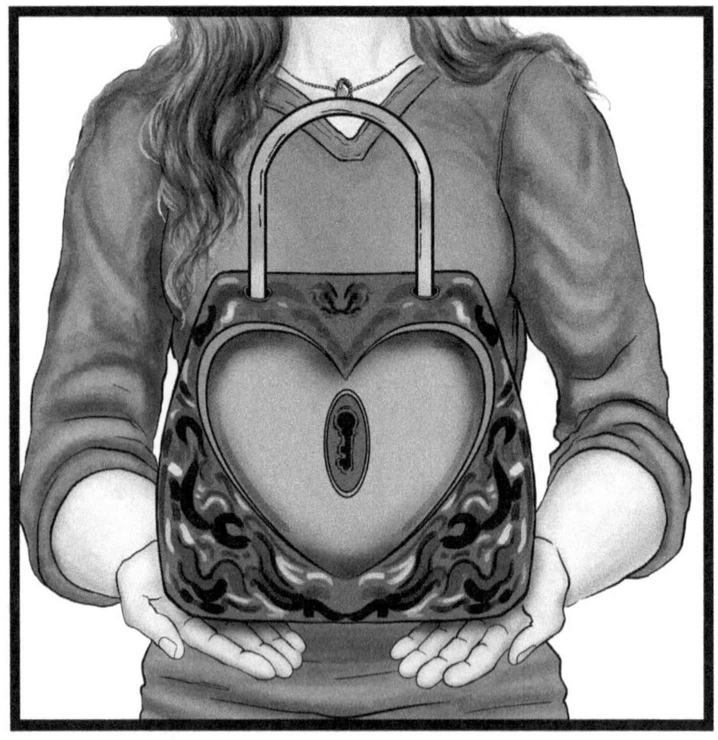

Then Lucas began retelling the story. The Sharefield Gang listened attentively despite having heard it before when they first met in Sharefield Park. Some pondered whether the key itself held special significance or if Lucas possessed the ability to see these strange double images. The gang had learned from their experiences over the past two years to keep an open mind. Jumping to conclusions too quickly could be dangerous.

Dion then shared the story of the old Commodore 64 computer as he pulled it out of his backpack. The gang tried to restart the computer that afternoon, but it would not respond, just like on the day when it suddenly stopped operating.

Lucas said, "Wow, so this was the computer in my dream that diagnosed me in the hospital. Who knows, there may be a medical journal on the back side of that Datasette tape. If we ever get this computer working again, we should check that out."

"That's an interesting thought," said Dion, as everyone laughed.

Then Lucia remarked, "I wonder if Lucas's key would have opened the briefcase containing the computer. I thought that Peter had the only other key."

"You are always thinking ahead," admired Anthony. There is so much to like about you. Then, there was silence within the group.

After a few seconds, Kim remarked, "Yes, that is right." And how did Ms. Brock end up with an identical key in the first place?"

Lucia asked Dion and Lucas if she could examine their keys. They both handed them to her. She placed one on top of the other and held them up for everyone to see. Anthony immediately remarked, "Wow, they are different!"

"Yes, they are different," said Nate. "Where have you been? We know the faces are different."

Anthony said, "No, look closely. Lucas's key is cut slightly different than Dion's. It would open a different lock." Everyone was astonished and wanted to examine the two keys for themselves.

"Sure enough," said Nate, "there's a slight difference in the cut of the two keys. Anthony is right. I am bewildered."

Lucia said, "I suspected that might be the case. We need to compare these keys to the one that Ms. Brock has."

"How are we going to do that?" said Kim. "I'm not sure," said Lucía, "but there is only a week left till the end of the school year, so we need to think of something fast."

"I don't see why she wouldn't show it to us if we ask her," said Chelsea.

"Yes, but we need to compare the cut to the two keys here. The difference may be subtle between the two keys," said Kim.

"You're right, Kim," said Chelsea, "that could be a big problem. Ms. Brock doesn't know about these other keys."

Then Dion added, "We do not want to tell her about them either, at least not at this time, not while we're trying to discover why our two keys are for different locks."

Nate asked, "Can we devise a way to get a picture of Ms. Brock's key? That is if we can get her to show it to us."

"Good idea!" said Dion. "But how will we pull that off? We need a reason to want to photograph her key. And we better get it done soon, given that we are near the end of the school year."

"I have an idea," said Lucia. "Barka played Wanna Noah in this year's production of *The Caribbean Adventure.* She's also on the yearbook committee. We know that Ms. Brock is very fond of that key and proud of its place in the Sharefield theater program. Perhaps, with Barka's help, we can convince Ms. Brock to let us have a picture of the key and an interview elaborating on its value as a theatrical icon for inclusion in our yearbook."

"Fantastic idea, that could work," said Anthony. "Once we have a picture, we can study the details of the key cut and compare it to the two other keys we have here. Lucia, you have done it again."

"Well, not so fast. We still need to pull this scheme off."

Nate responded, "Let'sLet's start by taking a picture of these keys for reference."

Anthony volunteered by pulling out his phone, the Silver Long Ranger, and snapped a few pictures of both Dion's and Lucas's keys.

The following morning, Lucia and Chelsea ran into Barka between classes and arranged to discuss matters further at lunch. There, they pitched the idea to Barka of featuring Ms.

Brock's 'theater key' in the yearbook, suggesting a photo and article about its significance. Barka was all in favor of the proposal.

After school that evening, the three girls approached Ms. Brock at her desk and presented their ideas. Ms. Brock agreed to a picture and a concise description of the key's value as an icon of past and future productions. However, she declined to provide the full history of the key for the yearbook.

She insisted that her brother be included in the writeup because of his intimate involvement in the school's past theater productions. "He is a wise old owl, you know," she told the girls.

With Barka's embroidered silk handkerchief as a backdrop, they photographed the key and recorded an interview with Ms. Brock.

Kim asked Ms. Brock an additional question, "Off the record, can you share with us how you came to have such a beautiful key?"

Ms. Brock remarked, "You know, I hardly remember. I have had this key since I was a little girl. I recall being at a large family reunion. There was a friendly old man there who knew my parents. He enjoyed playing with me and the other children, who I guess were some of my relatives, although not close cousins. I recall not knowing most of them. Anyway, we played a game I won, and this man gave me the key as a prize. I don't even remember what the game was or the man's name, but I kept the key all these years in my jewelry box because I thought it was pretty. Last year, when our school was rehearsing for the performance of *The Script,* I pulled the key out and decided that it would fit nicely into the production. I decided to use the key again since Jimmy wrote the play for this year's performance. I considered making it a standing tradition in our theater program, as I disclosed during my presentation at Diyton South Side."

"That is a fascinating story, Ms. Brock," said Kim. "Thank you for sharing it with us."

"Yes, and thank you for the picture of the key and the information you shared with us specifically for the yearbook," said Barka. "I'll provide you with an official copy of the write-up for your review before printing."

Ms. Brock said, "That would be a good idea. "I look forward to seeing how the yearbook comes together. I know you have diligently worked on it throughout the year."

Barka smiled and said, "This article will be a meaningful addition to this year's book."

As they left Ms. Brock's desk, Chelsea asked Barka if she could share the picture of the key with the promise that she wouldn't spoil the yearbook article. Barka, somewhat reluctantly, obliged and transferred the image to Chelsea's phone.

Chelsea commented after Barka left to edit the article from Ms. Brock, "We've helped the yearbook staff and got our picture of the key. That was clever work, I would say."

Kim agreed, "Let's get the gang back together in my base-ment tomorrow after school so we can all take a closer look at Ms. Brock's key and compare it to the others."

Nate and Lucas had soccer practice that afternoon, but the rest of the gang met at Kim's house. Chelsea showed the photo on her phone to Anthony, who had the other two pictures of Dion's and Lucas's keys. Anthony scrutinized both phones for a minute and then declared, "The cut on Ms. Brock's key differs from Dion's. It looks exactly like Lucas's key!"

Dion chimed in, "Well, that kind of makes sense since the key machine was supposed to make an exact copy of Ms. Brock's key. I wonder how it made one side different from the other?"

Lucia asked, "Did you learn anything else about Ms. Brock's key while speaking with her yesterday?"

"Yes, we did," said Chelsea. "She mentioned she was given the key as a child at a family reunion."

Around that time, Nate and Lucas arrived at Kim's house after soccer practice. The others explained the situation. Nate said, "We should call Victor out on the coast. Maybe he has a fresh perspective."

Victor was just getting home from school. He was happy to hear from his friends. Upon reviewing the situation, he said, "Well, since Dion's key opened a briefcase and Lucas's key is remarkably similar, maybe it's the key to a second briefcase. When I was in Sharefield with you, Ms. Brock mentioned that the old man who lived in the mansion was a distant relative.

You never know since she got the key as a little girl at a family reunion. Maybe there's a connection there."

Impressed by Victor's insight, Nate said, "I knew you could help us figure this out."

Kim pondered, "I wonder if we should contact Mr. and Mrs. Martinez and ask them about a second briefcase."

Lucia and Anthony visited the mansion the next day to inquire about a possible second briefcase. Ms. Claire Martinez was home that day and greeted them at the door. After being asked about a second briefcase, she responded, "I don't know of another one. I remember the disposal crew taking the first briefcase from the attic soon after we bought the place, but we have not seen another one since."

She then added, "I would remember seeing such an old briefcase that looks like a miniature suitcase. We cleared everything out of the house after you and your friends cleaned it. After adding a lot of new furnishings and keeping a few of the older pieces still in good shape, we have been renting the rooms ever since. No one has ever mentioned seeing a briefcase stuffed in a closet somewhere, or anywhere else for that matter. Surely, if there were something like that around here, it would have turned up by now."

Lucia and Anthony thanked Mrs. Martinez for her time and left disappointed with her assessment.

Anthony said to Lucia, "We must continue to chase this case of the missing one."

Lucia replied, "I agree. Maybe you should not make light of it."

"That is, unless there is nothing in it, and we come up empty-handed."

Smiling, Lucia said, "You are impossible."

Anthony seemed to enjoy her mild frustration with him.

7

THE GLASS TABLE

It was the end of the school year and time for the traditional trip to the Majestic Mountain waterfall to capture the annual class picture. The day was blustery and windy, leading to a comical scene as all the girls attempted to manage their hair before the photo.

After the picture, there was nothing scheduled back at school that day. The gang asked Ms. Jenkins if they could hike upstream to the bridge across the Wandering River. They secretly wanted to revisit the strange rock formation resembling a creature from another world they had encountered in one of their virtual reality sessions. Ms. Jenkins granted permission, asking everyone to return to the bus at 1:00 p.m. sharp for the trip back to school on time.

Hurrying to the bridge, the gang enjoyed reminiscing over the view of the Wandering River. They even snapped a picture of the rock formation below that now supported the bridge they stood upon. It was a memorable piece of their shared history. On returning to the bus, Anthony picked a wild daisy and handed it to Lucia. In a playful voice, she said, "Oh, thank you for the thoughtful gift from nature's florist," and put the flower in her hair for safekeeping.

In addition to the traditional class picture outing, the teachers arranged a special field trip to a design studio this year. The students would observe and participate firsthand in designing an actual product. While the gang wasn't sure about what to expect, they eagerly anticipated the opportunity.

Early Friday morning, the gang and others who had signed up for this offsite adventure piled onto the bus and headed to an undisclosed design studio. They rode just out of town until the bus pulled into the parking lot of a flat-roofed building. With no signs out front or on the sides of the building, few cars in the parking lot, and the brick walls painted a medium beige color, the building seemed almost unoccupied.

Approaching the glass door in front, the students found it covered top to bottom with a light impenetrable black cloth. It was clear that someone wanted to keep whatever was inside secret.

Mr. Thomas, the science teacher coordinating the expedition, walked up to the door and tried to open it. It was locked.

Beside the door was a handwritten sign that read, 'Please ring the bell'. Mr. Thomas pushed the antique-looking round bell button. Everyone listened, but no one heard a sound. After a couple of minutes, Mr. Thomas pressed the button again. This time, they heard a latch rattling inside the door before it slowly opened. Standing in front of them was a middle-aged man, thin, with nice hair. He greeted everyone with a smile, opened the door wide, and said, "Come on in."

What they encountered next defied comprehension for a gang that had grown up with many toys throughout their childhood. Stepping into the front lobby, a combined show-room of a most successful toy design firm, they saw a fan turning slowly on the ceiling. Around it were numerous multi-colored displays swinging back and forth as if they were alive. The entire room pulsed with excitement in unison, matching the wonder in the eyes of the students as they entered. It felt as though the space had been inhabited by fictitious creatures tailored specifically for the Sharefield Central High students.

Adorning the walls were futuristic works of art depicting characters with shapes and colors that were beyond imagination. To the left was a display case filled with some of the most peculiar-looking toys. From preschool blocks to dolls and action figures galore, the array included recognizable heartfelt memories the gang had played with as children. Others were far-out fantasy items that had a place only as outcasts of the most futuristic science fiction movies.

The gang and the rest of their classmates gazed in awe at the sheer variety and scale of the marinating creativity that lined the lobby walls, flavoring all the senses with imaginary color. One couldn't help but wonder: who could have envisioned all this in their most abstract dreams, let alone bring it to life physically, assembled here in one place?

Just then, a small robot, about a foot and a half tall, came rolling into the room. It announced itself, "Hello, I am Chipper. I am here to greet and escort you to our design center."

The person who had opened the door closed it behind the last student to enter, then walked ahead, following the robot. He instructed everyone to come along behind him. The gang knew they were in for an enchanting adventure. Chipper led the group down a long hallway adorned with painted characters on the walls, depicting exaggerated realism of all shapes and sizes.

Nate remarked to Dion, "I think that if there were such a thing as a toy character circus, the ones on this wall would be the stars of the show."

"Yes, I agree," said Dion. "What could possibly be next?"

Chipper and their host led them into a large, high-tech-looking room with an enormous rectangular-shaped glass table in the center. Then, Chipper scurried off into the corner and stood at attention while the host told everyone to sit at the table. The gang all sat together. Once everyone was situated, the man who brought them in stood at the head of the table, announcing that his name was Jason. He said he would lead the day's activities with his colleagues Olivia and Lin.

On cue, they both entered from a door to the left in the front of the room. Jason introduced them. They each shared their background and particular expertise with the students. All three hosts for the day had worked in toy design for many years. They were all quite accomplished, explaining that they had developed a multitude of toys that have been marketed throughout the years, including everything in their front showroom. The students were in awe of their portfolios.

There were chocolate chip cookies on the table. Jason offered everyone a drink and passed around a bottle opener, inviting the students to enjoy the refreshments.

Then, he announced that the class would collaborate with the professional designers throughout the day to develop their next toy. All the students were thrilled to participate in this exercise.

Lin said, "We want all of you to help us create a new toy from start to finish. Share your ideas, and together, we'll decide on something and move forward."

Excited chatter filled the room as everyone spoke at once about their ideas with each other.

Jason suggested, "Let's take turns around the table, one student at a time so that each of you can express your best idea while the rest listen."

Some toy design proposals sparked laughter as students threw out all sorts of mind-twisting ideas. Olivia diligently recorded them all on a whiteboard.

Once everyone had shared their ideas, Olivia said, "Now, let's bring some order to this chaos. Before we categorize these ideas, would anyone like to combine their idea with another to make an even stronger concept?"

The students examined the list on the board. Several noticed related ideas that could be combined, making the list a little shorter. Olivia then outlined some conditions that needed to be applied to the list. She referred to these as 'boundary conditions.'

"First of all, we want to design something new, so let's eliminate everything from the list developed in the past. Lin, Jason, and I together have a thorough understanding of the history of this industry, so we will cross off some of the items that resemble existing or previously marketed products."

The students were surprised at how many items were removed because of prior innovation.

Olivia continued, "Next, we need to eliminate the overly complex products and either difficult to design or too costly for the average consumer."

Anthony lamented, "Darn, there goes my Super Uber Duper Basketball that homes in on the basket with its laser tracking device without ever missing a shot."

Nate said with a smile, "Nice try, Anthony. I guess that you will just have to practice."

After the second set of eliminations, only a few items remained on the board.

Suddenly, a series of previously unnoticed screens pointing up at the glass table from underneath lit up and began displaying images. The screens started at one end and extended all the way down the length of the large banquet-sized conference room table. They were fully illuminated with rapidly flickering colors and changing images every few seconds. The light filtering through the glass above them gave the illusion of three-dimensional images.

Olivia explained, "Our visual assistant will help us with the design today. The screens in front of each of you will capture your voice and generate pictures of what you are discussing. As we evolve our designs, the intelligence behind the screens will update the images, allowing us to visualize them as we discuss the possibilities."

"This is so cool," said Chelsea.

Lucia chimed in, "I'm thinking we should create a doll that does homework." As Chelsea laughed, a doll with glasses and a pencil in hand appeared on the screen beneath her section of the table. The doll was writing and solving math problems on a piece of paper.

"Wow," gasped Lucia, "do you see that? The doll I described is right there on the screen below me, working on math problems."

Everyone watched with amazement. Olivia said, "You are experiencing the power of our design innovation system. It is quite capable, don't you agree?"

Everyone wanted to try the system out with the remaining ideas on the board. The students eagerly described the various attributes of their ingenious ideas. The screens updated with image variations at an incredible speed as the students unleashed the possibilities.

Olivia said, "Now that you've got the hang of it let's decide on one project to work on together. We have four promising candidates remaining on the board. They include:

1. A talking candy vending machine game.

2. A construction set made of chains and pipes.

3. Racing turtles.

4. A telescope with an electronic star generator."

There was considerable discussion around the table over the four items, with the screens below capturing and displaying the students' ideas throughout. After several minutes, Olivia paused the conversation as Lin activated a large display at the front of the room. He scrolled through all the images captured by the table displays for each of the four ideas. "

This is really quite astonishing," said Dion. As everyone reviewed the images for each concept, Olivia announced, "We can only choose one of them today, so let's take a vote to determine which one is the favorite."

The vote was so close, with racing turtles winning by a single vote. Anthony joked, "Once a turtle saved me, I voted for them to return the favor." Olivia said, "I'm not sure I fully understand that situation, but let's move on. Why did some of you other students vote for the turtles?"

One student replied, "Because I like competition." Another student remarked, "Because this concept has potential for design freedom and creative expression."

"Insightful," said Olivia. One student in particular who had a turtle as a pet asked, "Who doesn't like turtles?" Another had visited an aquarium and watched sea turtles swim in the large tank. Yet another had seen one down along the Wandering River. Olivia summed it up by saying, "The turtles are more than a toy. They are memories. They conjured up feelings given their emotional connection to many of your lives. That may translate to the lives of potential customers as well. This is part of what makes a superior product. So, the racing turtles it is."

"Now, let's get down to business," said Jason. Lin switched off all the screens and said, "First, we'll have a moment of silence so that you can visualize some aspect of this design in your mind. Please try to envision the finished product: How does it look? What does it do? What is so fascinating about it?"

After a brief pause, Lin reactivated the screens back on and instructed the students to describe their visions. He stated, "The screens will reflect your ideas."

The system worked perfectly, like a symphony with all the instruments in tune. Ideas melded together like the gears on a massive antique grandfather clock. Soon, the screen displayed multiple images of turtles at the starting line of a race, ready to face off against each other. As Olivia moderated the discussion, various attributes of the assorted designs were fused into two hot, saucy turtles that looked ready for the Grand Prix. Lin showcased the finalized designs on the large screen at the front of the room.

"This is incredibly satisfying," remarked Chelsea. Lucia nodded in agreement, while Anthony acknowledged, "This design is so much better than my Super Uber Duper Basketball."

"Okay," said Jason, "let's gear up for the race. First, we'll need to figure out some control functions, but before we do that, we should give each turtle a name."

The students started throwing out names all at once. "I suggest we give one a female name and the other a male name," said Olivia. Going around the room, she ended up with a host of submissions.

When she asked Anthony, he replied, "I think we should call one of them 'Turt'. Turt is rough, tough, and ready for a battle on the racecourse,"

Lucia was sitting beside him, so she went next. She offered the other should be called 'Tella'. "Tella is competitive, strategic, spunky, and has a sixth sense for racing."

"Okay," said Olivia, "I am not sure that turtles already have the other five senses, but that does not matter for this exercise." Those two names remained the overwhelming favorites among the students, hence becoming the ultimate choices. Lin added the two names to everyone's screen.

"Can we decorate their shells?" asked Lucia.

"Why certainly," said Olivia. "It'll add to their personalities. What do you suggest?" Lucia proposed putting flowers on Tella.

"How about daisies?" asked Kim.

"Yes," said Chelsea.

"Daisies for Tella it is," said Olivia.

Anthony suggested, "I like lightning bolts for Turt so that he looks fast." Everyone agreed that was a desirable choice.

Olivia asked, "Now we need to figure out how to control these racers."

Chelsea said, "I don't think we should confine them to a specific track. How about we just set out some markers around the play area to define the racecourse of the moment and then have Turt and Tella track to those markers? This way, the child playing the game can interact more with the racers. They can configure the raceway to their individual play space."

"That is an excellent idea," said Olivia, "consider it done."

Lin explained, "We have done something similar before and have the technology in hand to manage tracking the markers, as long as the turtles are not running so fast that they're unable to correct their direction along the route between markers."

Then Nate asked, "What will distinguish one racer from the other? Won't they both just move from marker to marker in a similar way?"

"Another very good question," said Olivia. "What are some obvious ways of discriminating one racer from another?"

Dion replied, "Speed and agility?"

"Good!" said Olivia. "It's difficult to have both at the same time." One of the other students suggested configuring a single control knob for both. "Turn it one way, and you get maximum speed. Turn it in the other direction and you get the best maneuverability."

"I like that," Kim remarked. "This way, the child can adjust to any combination of speed and agility based on how they have set up the racecourse."

Kim leaned over and said to Dion, "We think a lot alike."

Dion replied, "We make a good turtle design team."

Jason suggested, "The more the user can interact with the turtles, the more personal the toy becomes for them. As a result, they will like your racing turtles all the more." Then he asked, "Are these the only controls we need for these racers?"

Dion thought about it, then said, "There's still something missing. What we have so far is good for one turtle racing around the course, but what about the competitive element between Turt and Tella? We need a way for them to interact with each other during the race."

"Another compelling insight," said Olivia. "Does anyone have an idea?" Anthony spoke up, "Why don't we create controls for offense and defense, similar to strategies used in different sports? It could control how our friendly turtles interact."

"What do you mean," asked Olivia, "Can you be more specific?"

"I don't know," said Anthony. "I guess a more offensive player would actively try to collide with the other turtle, whereas a more defensive player would swiftly try to evade a collision."

"Yes," said Lucia, "an offensive turtle could have the ability to quickly change speeds to disrupt the other turtle's progress, while a defensive player may have the ability to quickly roll over and keep going if hit by the opposing turtle. We can use a single dial, like the speed and agility dial. Turning it to one end can offer maximum offense while turning it opposite increases defensive capability. Each dial can be set to the combination the child wants before each race begins."

"This is a captivating approach," said Olivia, with Lin and Jason concurring. Lin said, "Now that our racing turtles are defined, we should run through a simulation to see how they perform." He inputs the parameters into the simulation program, and all the screens under the glass table show Turt and Tella at the starting line, ready to race.

Jason said, "They're ready, everyone, count to three." As the count reached three, Turt and Tella shot off at hyper speed on a simulated course, weaving around furniture, darting under a coffee table, and finally crossing the finish line marked by a checkered flag in a kitchen doorway. It was an exhilarating race, with one turtle rolling over the other as they negotiated sharp turns through the room with utmost precision.

The room erupted in cheers, like a homecoming football game. The students were elated with the design they had created that day.

That morning, when they first arrived at the design studio, they had no idea what they were about to achieve. As they prepared to leave, they realized they had accomplished something extraordinary by working together as a team. The collective wisdom of the group surpassed the capabilities of any single student.

Jason thanked them all for their participation. He told the students that the professional design team was particularly impressed with their creative spirit. He concluded by saying, "By working together, you developed an exciting new toy that fully engages children. You are giving them control over setting up their own course, negotiating it, and interacting with the other racing turtle. Your toy empowers children to explore," he explained. "This accomplishment evolved from a series of ideas. Your future is similar. You can chart your course and develop the skills needed to negotiate all the twists and turns it will present. Make the most of those dials in your head as you design your own personal turtle race. Just like Turt and Tella, you're all off to the races."

As the students boarded the bus to return to school, each felt a personal sense of satisfaction in their accomplishments for the day. The empowerment imparted to the child through their toy was transferred to, and emotionally felt by, each of them. They gained confidence, knowing that if they could design racing turtles as remarkable as Turt and Tella, they could accomplish many other outstanding things through analysis and teamwork.

On the bus, Nate said, "We should adopt a turtle as our soccer team mascot." The gang couldn't wait to tell Lucas about their day's adventure. Anthony made up an impromptu turtle song while everyone sang along. It went like this:

Kick fast the class that invented two tumbling turtles.

They roll and they rumble, they rock, and they tumble.

Racing to the end victory they defend.

Go, Go Turt our favorite turtle fella, and Miss Tella our turtle blissful Bella!

After singing along with everyone. Lucia sat quietly amid the noisy chatter. She was conflicted.

Ever since she was a little girl, she wanted to be a seamstress and clothing designer. She would sketch new clothing designs over the figures in her coloring book and then masterfully color them in beautiful complementary shades. It felt as though this talent coursed through her veins. She really excelled at creating contemporary designs for the school theater productions and always received accolades for her work. Yet, as she soaked in the creative energy of the design studio, she felt bewildered.

She thought, *There are an overwhelming number of possibilities in front of me. Can I design consumer products or get involved in interior design?* She knew she had a good eye for how things coordinate to be aesthetically pleasing. Suddenly, her eyes were opened to a host of new possibilities.

She thought further to herself, *I don't have to make any decisions today, but it's certainly something new worth considering. I really liked what we did today and think I'd be good at this sort of thing. Or perhaps it would be fun to try to design a living space from start to finish. The inside of that design studio inspired me to think of interior design. I will fill the pages of my sketchbook with designs beyond just clothing, expressing my creativity in new and exciting ways.*

Anthony noticed that Lucia was withdrawn and appeared to be introspective. When she finally looked up, he said to her, "Did you leave the bus for a turtle trip to a distant land?"

Lucia smiled and said, "Something like that, only closer to home." Anthony did not quite understand, but he sensed that she wanted to keep her thoughts private for the moment, so he did not question her further.

8

CHANGES IN SHAREFIELD

As the weekend approached, and the school year drew to a close, Nate and Lucas started looking forward to playing together on the select soccer team over the summer. Saturday morning brought them together for their next practice session at Sharefield Park. When Lucas arrived, the band was practicing as it had done for the past several weeks. Pausing briefly to soak in the music, Lucas eventually joined the team for practice. The band members couldn't help but notice his interest in their melodies.

After practice, Nate invited Lucas to grab some ice cream and sit in the park with the rest of the Sharefield Gang. Lucas gladly accepted, given that he would have an extra hour before his mom was to pick him up. Gathering around their favorite oak tree, the gang was bustling with excitement, eager to talk to Lucas. They shared every detail of their exciting field trip to the design studio, where they created Turt and Tella from thin air. Lucas was fascinated by their turtle tale. He said, "I wish I had more time to spend with you here in Sharefield."

He pulled out his key and told everyone it was their bond. Lucas suddenly noticed something peculiar about his key – a screw image appeared to be protruding from its surface. He turned the key over and saw that the screw was on top of an ice cream cone, just like the one he had just finished eating. "What could this mean?" he said, passing the key to Nate.

Nate inspected the key but did not see anything special. "What do you mean, my friend? I see a key and nothing more, as usual." He returned the key to Lucas, who said, "Yeah, I don't see anything now either. I swore I saw a screw that became the ice cream on a cone a minute ago. This is so confusing."

Chelsea replied, "A screw is usually used to hold things together."

"Or to fix something," added Dion. "Do you know of anything that's broken?"

Lucas remembered seeing his bicycle that morning as his mother put on her sunglasses and pulled the car out of the garage to take him to soccer practice. She said something about the morning sun being rather bright. Lucas was just announcing to the gang that his bike was broken when a picture of a pair of glasses appeared on the key.

"That's strange," said Lucas, now I see a pair of glasses." He quickly flipped the key over and saw the glasses transform into a bicycle. "Now there's a bicycle on the key."

Everyone got up and stood behind Lucas to get a look for themselves, but by the time they gathered to see, the images had vanished.

"As always," Lucas sighed, "it was just there, and now it is gone."

Chelsea remarked, "We believe you, Lucas. You see what you see in your own mind. We cannot dispute that."

Lucas was not sure what to make of the comment.

As the time neared for Lucas's mother to arrive, Lucia had a sudden idea. "You know, it's only ten miles between Diyton and Sharefield. The bike trail runs along the old railroad tracks connecting the two towns. You could make that trip on your bike in a little over a half-hour, give or take a few minutes."

"That's an interesting idea," said Kim. Lucas nodded in agreement. "Yeah, it is. I haven't ridden my bike in a few years, but maybe I could fix it. Then, I could spend more time here with all of you and not be so dependent on my parents' schedule. There's a bike shop in Diyton. The old man who runs the shop is an excellent mechanic. Wait a minute, he wears glasses like the ones I just saw in the key." Lucas's mom arrived at the park just then, calling for him. He jumped up and ran toward her, ready to head back to Diyton.

By the middle of the following week, Lucas had taken his bike in for repairs and returned it from the shop in perfect condition. He was excited about the prospect of commuting to Sharefield whenever he wanted to spend time with his new friends there.

That evening at dinner, prompted by rather unusual weather reports on the news, Lucas's parents were discussing the climate changes and how these extremes were affecting the ecosystem. The conversation left an impression on Lucas, who began to ponder what the environment might be like when he was older.

Later that night, before bed, he took his key out of his pocket and examined it closely before placing it on his nightstand. All the lights in his room were on.

Suddenly, he noticed what seemed to be an image of a fork emanating from the center of the key. He rubbed his eyes and looked again, thinking it might be his tired imagination. *No, he thought, I'm certain that I see a fork.* By now, he had learned to trust the key and its messages. Quickly, he turned the key over and saw the fork transform into a plug being inserted into an electrical socket.

What could this possibly mean? he thought to himself, before drifting off to sleep. The following morning, he grabbed the key off his nightstand as the sun pierced through the window. What he saw left him dumbfounded. There was a cinnamon roll in the center of his key. The kind he would really like to have for breakfast, given how hungry he was.

Perplexed, he turned the key over and observed that delicious, warm, doughy cinnamon roll transformed into a roll of hay in a field. Lucas just shook his head in dismay as he sat the key back down on his nightstand and began to get dressed.

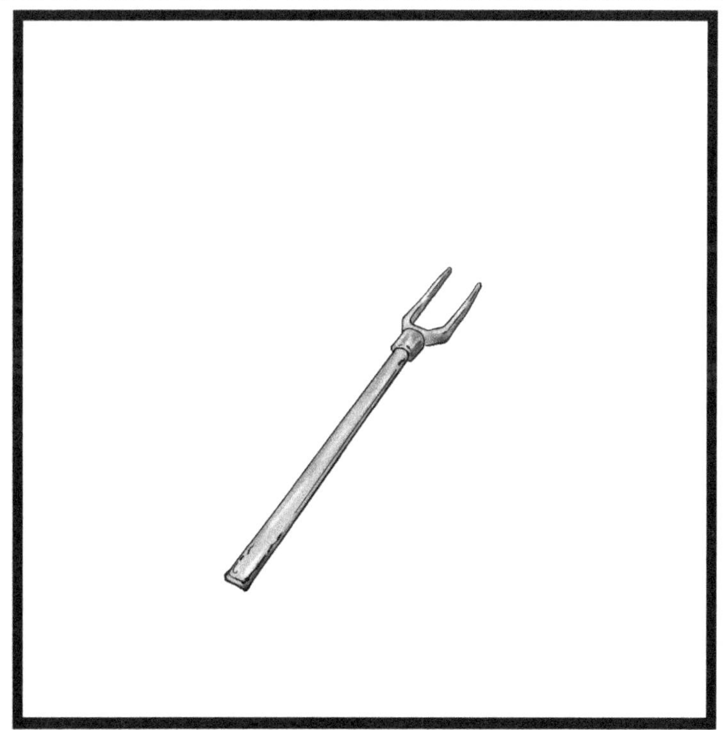

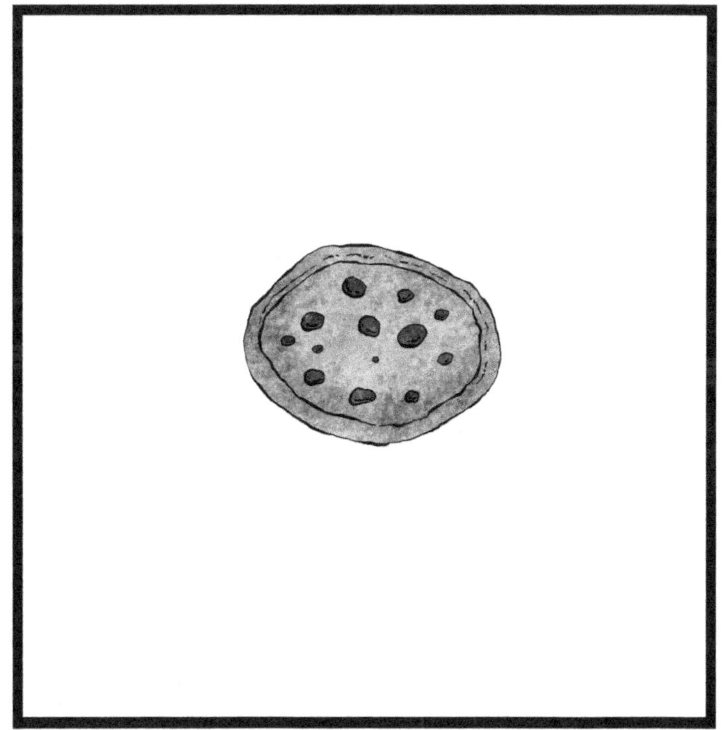

Uncertain of what to make of it all, he picked up the key once again. This time, he saw a dinner roll in the middle of the key. *This is becoming almost comical,* he thought to himself as he flipped the key into the air like the coin toss at a soccer game. He caught the key with the opposite side facing upward in his hand. The dinner roll had transformed into a hat on a chef. *Perhaps something to do with working in a bakery. These last several image pairs must relate to the same thing, but I have no idea what it is,* he thought.

Lucas was thrilled to ride his newly reconditioned bike to Sharefield after school. It was the last day of classes for both Diyton South Side and Sharefield Central. The gang would gather in Kim's basement to celebrate, and he was invited. School let out early that day after everyone turned in their books and bid goodbye to their teachers and friends they wouldn't see over the summer. Before Lucas hopped on his bike for the ride along the bike path to Sharefield, he pulled the key out of his pocket to check it once again.

This time there was a picture of a chocolate chip cookie projected from the key. *More bakery stuff,* he thought to himself. As he turned the key over, he saw the cookie become a pizza about to go into an oven.

I wonder what the gang will think of this when I meet up with them this afternoon and tell them about all of these latest images. Lucas thought to himself.

He put the key back in his pocket, jumped on his bike, and set out for Sharefield. He had not been on that trail before. He wasn't sure what to expect.

Once he got out of Diyton City proper, he was elated. The trail was paved and well-marked. It was wide enough for three bikes across. Trees lined the trail on both sides. The wooded surroundings opened in random intervals into vast fields of farmland with an occasional old farmhouse and classic red barn.

He relished the ride, finding it effortless. Lucas was in excellent shape. Pedaling along, he mused to himself, "What a great invention; pedaling is a lot easier than running." The sense of independence was overwhelming. About four miles out of Sharefield, things took a strange turn. A deep rumble, seeming to come from all sides, filled the air. He felt off balance as if the earth was shifting beneath him. It lasted only a few seconds before everything returned to normal.

What just happened, he thought. *Was that possibly an earthquake?*

From there on into Sharefield, he rode a bit slower, constantly looking around and keenly observing his surroundings. As he approached the town, his ears caught the numbing frequency of an emergency siren buried within the sound of the wind roaring past his ears. As he got closer, he could tell the high-decibel distress signal was broadcast from a large speaker atop a telephone pole along the bike trail. At that point, he was sure that something catastrophic had happened.

Soon, he arrived at Kim's house. The rest of the gang was already downstairs in her basement. They all had felt the shift in the earth and heard the piercing siren. The news was already being reported on multiple channels. Everyone was talking about it. It was confirmed to be a small earthquake centered on the edge of Sharefield. No one in that little town had ever experienced anything like that before.

Chelsea said to Lucas, "We're so glad you made it. Did you feel anything on the bike trail as you approached Sharefield?"

"I sure did," said Lucas. "I almost lost my balance a couple of times. It was an eerie feeling."

"The earthquake was not a devastating one, according to early reports, but intense enough to cause some serious damage, I'm certain," said Nate. "I wonder just how much was damaged around town," added Lucia. "I guess we will find out more in the following days."

"I just hope we don't have another one," Anthony said. "It is common for aftershocks to happen after something like this," said Lucia. "Often, the earth resettles itself after such a big shift."

"Since there's nothing we can do about it, let's get our minds off of this," said Kim.

"Lucas," she continued, "let me tell you about our other field trip this year. Our class got our picture taken, as is the tradition, under the falls of the Wandering River. It was a marvelous day, so the gang and I hiked upstream all the way to the bridge over the river. Anthony surprised us by playing the harmonica, and we sang along. It was a most enjoyable day." Lucas replied, "It's nice you got two field trips this year. Turt and Tella sound like a good match for each other.

I would not mind having a pair of those racing turtles myself to play with."

"You never know," said Lucia. "As we left the studio that day, Jason said that we did such an incredible job that their team is considering making an actual toy racing pair like the ones our class developed."

Anthony interjected, "If that were to happen, I would be the commentator and call out all the races."

"Just as you did with seahorse races?" questioned Dion.

"What seahorse races?" responded Lucas.

"That's another story," replied Chelsea. Then she asked Lucas if Diyton South Side had any end-of-year traditions. Lucas said, "Well, we had an impromptu talent show at the end of this year. It is not really a sanctioned affair, with parents in attendance. We all went to the gym on the assigned day. Anyone in the school interested in performing could get up on stage and entertain the rest of their classmates. It was a lot of fun.

"This year, we had two comedians and a dance couple. They were all incredible. Since I've been taking guitar lessons, I took my guitar that day just in case I might get a chance to play. One of the girls in my class brought a clarinet, and her friend was there with a tambourine. So, the three of us dared to hit the stage in front of everyone and play together. None of us had ever done anything like that before, but I have to say, it came off well. We did a couple of songs and got a standing ovation from the other students and the teachers alike. I never considered myself a musician, but when everyone was clapping and cheering for us, it sure did feel good."

"You must be exceptionally talented," said Chelsea, "maybe you can play for us someday. I would enjoy listening to you. Do you sing as well?"

"Yes, I sing as well. As well as a bullfrog. But I can sing through my fingers and let the guitar do the talking." said Lucas.

Lucas was reluctant to share the recent flurry of images he had seen in the key. He understood how peculiar it all must seem to the gang despite their accounts of past experiences with similar-looking keys. He remained perplexed that no one else could see the images that he saw. *"Perhaps they think it's me, not the key, causing these strange sightings,"* he pondered.

Nonetheless, he trusted his own perception. He couldn't stop looking at the key because it intrigued him. There was no guessing what he might find next inside its shiny decorative face.

He pulled it from his pocket and held it out in front of him. To his surprise, he saw a tambourine. He quickly turned it over and watched the tambourine become a trampoline. He thought about the stories the gang had told him. Then, he specifically remembered their virtual reality sessions and Dion's contraption.

Lucas realized how much the gang's friendship meant to him and how those relationships were influencing his life. He was thinking about all the experiences the gang shared with him. They reaffirmed to him that *Friendship is a choice, and I am happy with mine.*

As he glanced at the key again, he saw a daisy, then flipped it over to see that delicate flower become a ceiling fan, reminiscent of the gang's description of their trip to the design studio. He mused to himself, *Life is so full of surprises. There's so much to learn and discover.*

9

THE COMMUNITY UNITES

The first barbeque of the summer was scheduled to take place in two weeks at a farmhouse owned by Ms. Jenkins' parents.

On the morning of the event, Nate called his friend Victor. The two reminisced about the barbeque the year before, where Dion shot off his model rocket. Victor remembered how clever Lucia was in figuring out how to get the rocket launcher to work. Nate replied, "She really came up with an insightful solution that day." They exchanged their goodbyes just before Nate headed out for the barbeque.

The gang told Lucas he was welcome to ride together to the event in Kim's mom's spacious van. Lucas felt a strong sense of belonging and was delighted to be included. As they picked up Nate and the others in Sharefield, Kim's mom drove towards Diyton. Lucas was watching golf on TV when the van pulled into his drive. He hurriedly turned off the TV and ran out to greet his friends. Although golf wasn't a sport he played, he enjoyed staying updated on major sporting events.

It was a picture-perfect day for the barbecue, with no cloud in sight. On the way there, Nate told the others about his call with Victor. Lucas discreetly retrieved his key from his pocket and held it to his side. He was seated next to the window so the others could not see the key. He had established a routine of checking it several times a day, never knowing when it might reveal an image to him.

This time, even with the sunlight streaming through the car window, he could see a computer mouse in the key. Turning subtly to the other side, he saw the mouse become a luggage carrier on top of a vehicle.

Without a word to the others, he quickly slid the key back into his pocket before anyone could notice.

After they arrived at the barbeque and were strolling toward the picnic tables where the food was being prepared, Kim turned to Lucas and said, "Hey Lucas, do you have your key with you?"

Lucas replied, "Yes, I always carry it with me. It's become sort of a good luck charm."

"Do you see anything in it right now?" Lucas reluctantly pulled the key back out of his pocket. Then he replied, "No, not at this moment." The image he had seen just a brief time ago was gone. Lucas held the key up for the others to see and returned it to his pocket. He wanted to tell his friends about the several bakery-related images he had seen recently in the key, but this was not the time. He decided he could bring it up later that day at the barbeque.

This year's event seemed grander than the last. The entire town enjoyed being outdoors on a farm amid open fields and fresh air. The chatter among the Sharefield town residents was all about the earthquake that had disrupted their quiet lives just a few days before. No one knew what to make of it, with many questions swirling around.

"Would there be another one?"

"How extensive were the damages?"

"Where exactly did it originate?"

"Did everyone hear the warning siren that went off right after the first tremor?"

One lady remarked that she was doing the laundry when she heard the siren and, not knowing what was happening, ran for cover in the downstairs bathtub. She assumed it must be a tornado or another weather-related event blowing through town.

There were certainly a lot more questions than answers at that juncture. After everyone had eaten, Mr. Granzo stood up to make an announcement. The town knew him as the owner of the Mustang Pizzeria. He shared that his building had suffered structural damage during the recent quake and could not be salvaged.

"It will be heartbreaking to let go of a place that I've worked so hard to build into a thriving business," he said. "My heart and soul are in that place, but it is only brick and wooden tables. I vow to rebuild it even better for all the patrons of our fine community."

Everyone cheered. Chelsea's dad raised a toast to Mr. Granzo, saying, "My daughter and I have only lived here in Sharefield for a year or so, but we have felt the warmth that emanates from your family restaurant. Whenever Chelsea and her friends want a place to talk and enjoy a great meal, they always go for 'pizza at the pony,' the loving name they've given to your place. I believe that I speak for everyone here, saying that we will support you in any way we can in the reconstruction of your new restaurant."

The outpouring of support from the town was overwhelming, with several cash donations made on the spot, making it clear that the Mustang Pizzeria would once again thrive in Sharefield.

Mr. Granzo remarked, "The first order of business is to clear out the debris and salvage what I can from the existing structure. It's not going to collapse on its own, so it is safe to work inside. Eventually, it will need to be torn down and rebuilt."

The gang began talking among themselves about helping Mr. Granzo. "After all," said Kim, "we have some experience cleaning up buildings." She was referring to the old mansion that they helped with last summer. The gang told Lucas all about it, including the landscaping work they did around the grounds of the huge mansion. He was quite impressed.

They agreed that Dion would approach Mr. Granzo to offer the gang's services. The friends wanted to spend a few days at the pizzeria they had all come to love. They had plenty of good memories from that place and wanted to relive them one last time in the old building before its demolition. Mr. Granzo was grateful and readily accepted Dion's proposal to help. Lucia commented, "This is a great way for us to start our summer."

Soon after that, the dinner bell rang, signaling that all the food was ready and it was time to eat. The entire farm was engulfed with the treasured smoky fragrance of freshly cooked barbeque mixed with a plethora of smells from a variety of food that the town's people had lovingly prepared for this annual event. It was a time to celebrate community.

The gang fixed their plates and gathered at one of the picnic tables arranged in rows across an open field. The atmosphere was joyful. A special bond existed between the townspeople as they gave thanks for their safety despite the recent quake that had shaken the town.

Chelsea and Lucia poured themselves a cup of sweet peach tea. Chelsea remarked, "This tea is so tasty, but the flies seem to like it as much as I do." Lucia agreed, saying, "I don't know where they're coming from, but they seem to be jumping around my hand as I wave it in front of my glass as if playing a game with me." Anthony picked up a coaster and said, "Here, place this on top of your glass." Lucia took the flat cardboard coaster from Anthony with a pleasant, "Thank you, my friend."

Reminiscent about last year's event, Nate realized that the food tasted amazing. He thought to himself, *There is something about being out in the fresh air, combined with the feeling of a unified community, that is intensifying the smells and heightening the taste of all these homemade comfort dish specialties.*

After a delectable meal, the gang decided to walk through the vast farmland surrounding them.

Before Lucas rose from the picnic table, he took a quick peek at his key once again. This time, he saw a golf tee on the front side of the key, which became a clarinet on the flip side. He smiled, thinking, *Now there is a golfer that blows his own horn.* Just then, Nate, walking away, yelling back to him, "Come on, Lucas we are going exploring." He quickly stuffed his key into his pocket, jumped up, and joined his friends for the walk.

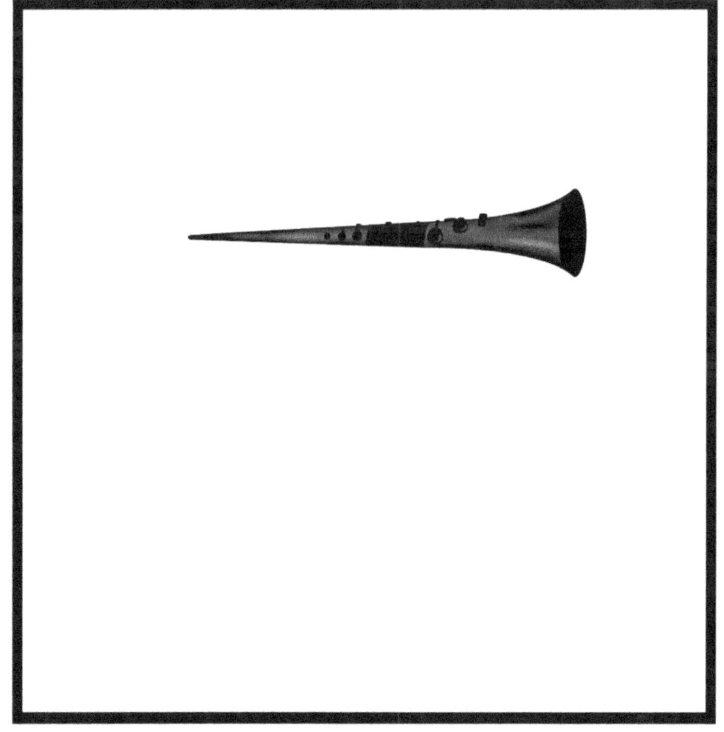

They strolled along the fence line, where the cows remained contently nestled inside, showing no desire to explore the world beyond their enclosure. Anthony said, "This is so relaxing; I could walk here with my friends until the cows come home."

"That would be at milking time," said Lucia.

Then Nate spotted something. He often scanned the path while walking and would generally be the first to spot a coin or any other object lying on the ground. What he saw this time was a strange-shaped rock. It appeared to have been man-made, but it was so old and dirty that no one could identify it with any certainty. "Let's take this back and clean it up," Nate suggested.

When the gang returned to the picnic area, they showed the rock to Ms. Jenkins' dad, who examined it carefully. He said, "What you have here is an arrowhead carved by the Cheroke Indians who inhabited these parts many years ago. This is an incredibly special piece you've found here."

Nate cleaned it up with some water to get the mud off. It was flint with hues of red, green, and gray. A very nice-looking piece. Ms. Jenkins' dad told the gang that the Indians used these arrowheads on spears and arrows shot from a bow in war and for hunting.

"How were they made?" asked Dion. Ms. Jenkins' dad replied, "First, they were chipped with a larger hard stone. This type of rock naturally chips with sharp edges because of its internal structure. Then the arrowheads were typically further sharpened using the antler of a deer or an elk."

"Wow," said Kim. "The Indians were very resourceful, weren't they? I believe they also realize that striking two pieces of flint against each other gave off sparks so they could be used to start a fire."

"That is absolutely correct," interjected Ms. Jenkins.

"You mean to tell me that they didn't even have matches with the Mustang Pizzeria logo on them?" said Anthony. "Life must have been hard back then."

"Or an electric rocket launcher that ran off of batteries," said Dion jokingly. Everyone laughed as Nate added, "You should have been here last year, Lucas."

The barbeque proved to be a light-hearted day for all. Although he intended to, Lucas never really got around to telling the gang about the latest images he had seen in his key. He figured he would have the opportunity the following day. He planned to ride his bike along the trail to Sharefield and meet up with the gang in the park. It was the girls' first softball game of the season. Chelsea was on the team playing first base, along with Kim, the pitcher.

That evening, before bed, Lucas saw a barrage of images in his key. They all related to the day's activities at the picnic somehow. It was overwhelming for Lucas. This was by far the most he had ever seen in his key since it dropped into the delivery bin in the machine at the hardware store. He thought to himself, *I must make it a point to discuss this with the gang tomorrow.*

Lucas was especially eager for the softball game in the morning, as Sharefield's team was playing against the Diyton girls' team, so Lucas knew many of the players. The rest of the gang showed up to watch the game as well. Anthony joked about eating peanuts and crackerjacks, given that all that was available at the small concession stand were a few canned drinks and some candy.

Unlike last year, the Sharefield girls were no match for their opponents from Diyton – they lost four to one. After the game, Kim said, "It's just the season's first game. Maybe we were all a bit nervous. I know I was. We lost the first game last year as well. We still have the whole summer ahead of us." Chelsea nodded in agreement, saying, "We'll do better as we learn to play together more and gel as a team."

After the game, the Sharefield Gang gathered under their favorite oak tree in the park. They wanted to talk about their commitment to help Mr. Granzo clean up the Mustang Pizzeria and recover items of value that survived the earthquake. Before they could start, Lucas pulled out his key and held it up for everyone to see.

"I'm still carrying it," he said before sharing the images he had been seeing in it. Top of Form

"You must believe me," he said. "I've been seeing several double images in this key that I want to reveal to you. It may seem a bit suspicious, but based on your experiences with similar keys, you have to trust me that there is something strangely different about this copper and zinc alloy that we call brass, which has been formed into this odd double-sided key. The images I see are all connected to our lives in one way or another. Eventually, with some reflection, I am generally able to understand their significance, with a few exceptions."

"You certainly have a point about magical keys from our past," said Kim. "We are all ears."

Lucas continued, "One evening after dinner before I was about to make my first ride to Sharefield, I saw a fork that became an electrical plug entering a socket. Perhaps that was the shocking news of what was about to be an earthquake. My parents had been discussing the potential effects of changes in the weather at dinner earlier that evening. Then I saw a series of images related to baked goods, including a dinner roll that turned into a baker's hat, a cinnamon roll in a hay field, and the most mysterious of all, a chocolate chip cookie that morphed into a pizza going into the oven. What could all this mean?"

Dion replied, "Perhaps you are somehow seeing things into the future through this key."

"Maybe," said Lucas. "I'm certain these images are all related to our lives."

He continued. "Next, the key showed a tambourine like the one at the impromptu school performance at Diyton South Side that transformed into a trampoline. I thought of the contraption that Dion described from your Lost View virtual reality sessions. Then I saw a flower, specifically a daisy, that became a ceiling fan after you told me about your trip to the design studio. Then, there was a computer mouse that became a car carrier. Most recently, I saw a girl playing a golf tee clarinet."

"How could the golf tee relate to anything we are familiar with?" said Nate. "I'm not sure, but I was watching golf on TV when Kim's mom picked me up before the Sharefield barbeque."

"Maybe I am seeing visions into the future, but I have also seen the past as well. After Lucia told us she was trying to comb her hair in the wind before your class photoshoot last week, I saw a comb that turned into a hedge trimmer, reminding me of the story you told me about the hedge you guys trimmed at the mansion last year."

"When we got home from yesterday's outing, I went to bed early and was hit with so many images that related to the events of the day. They just kept streaming one after another. I had no idea what was causing this enhanced activity, but the key was extremely hyperactive indeed. I didn't sleep well at all last night.

"Just what did you see?" asked Kim. "Well, first, I saw a loudspeaker that might project a warning siren. It turned into a washing machine."

Chelsea said, "I remember a lady at the picnic saying she was doing laundry when the siren warning of the earthquake went off. "Oh yes," said Anthony, "she hid in the bathtub."

"Yes, and then I saw a dustpan that became a glass used for a toast, as the one Chelsea's dad raised to Mr. Granzo, whose restaurant we will help clean up. This was followed by a fly swatter that transformed into a tea bag in a glass."

"We all know the symbolism of that one," said Lucia, as everyone laughed.

"That was not the end of it either," said Lucas. "Next, I saw an arrow fly." Nate looked around to make sure that nothing was coming at him. Lucas continued, "No, a fly like the annoying ones around the tea, and it became the fletching of an arrow. This one was quickly followed by a spear that became a lit candle like the fire that could be made from the flint rocks."

"Wow, that is a lot, my friend," said Chelsea. "No wonder you did not sleep much last night."

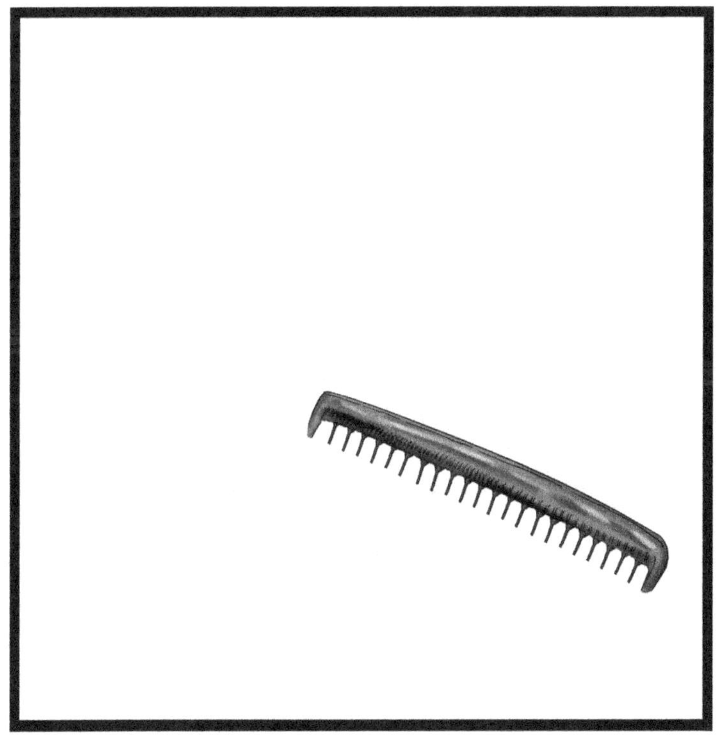

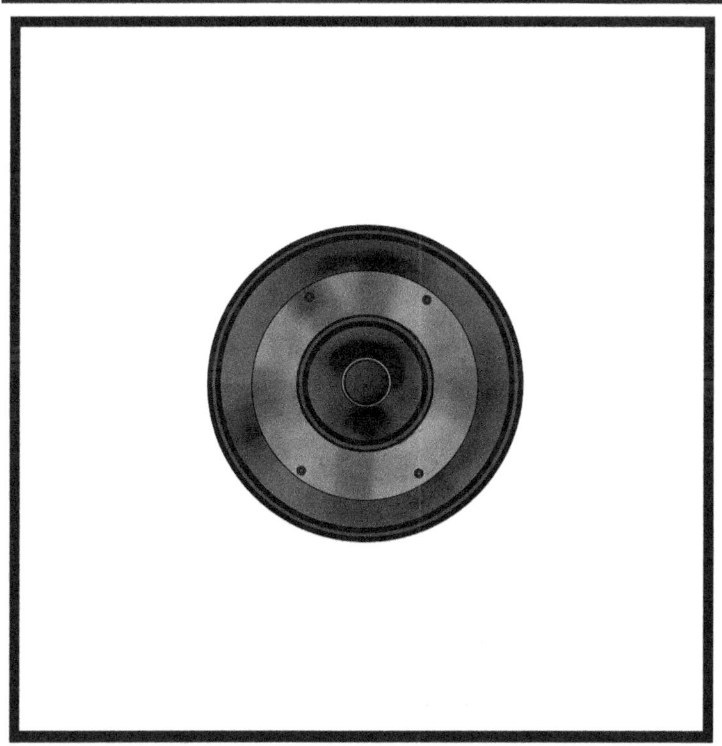

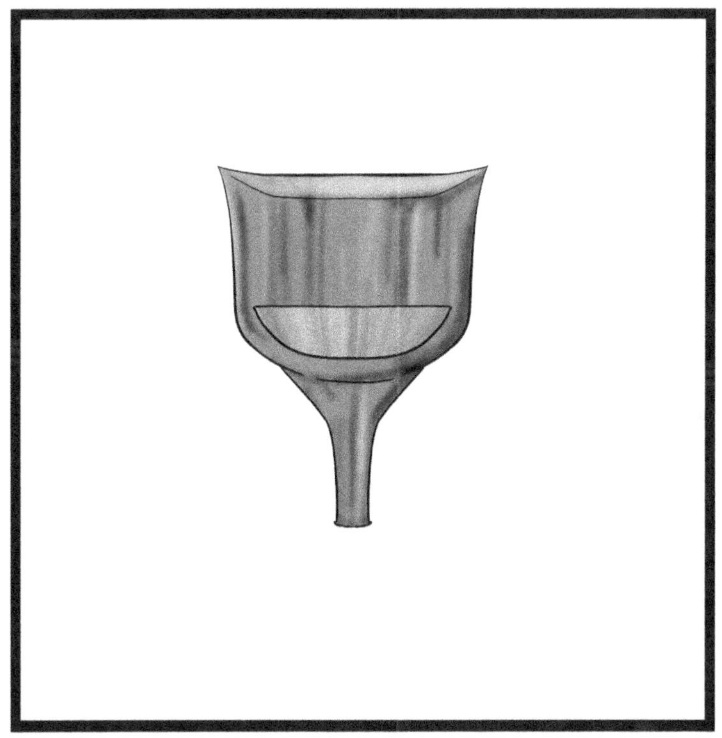

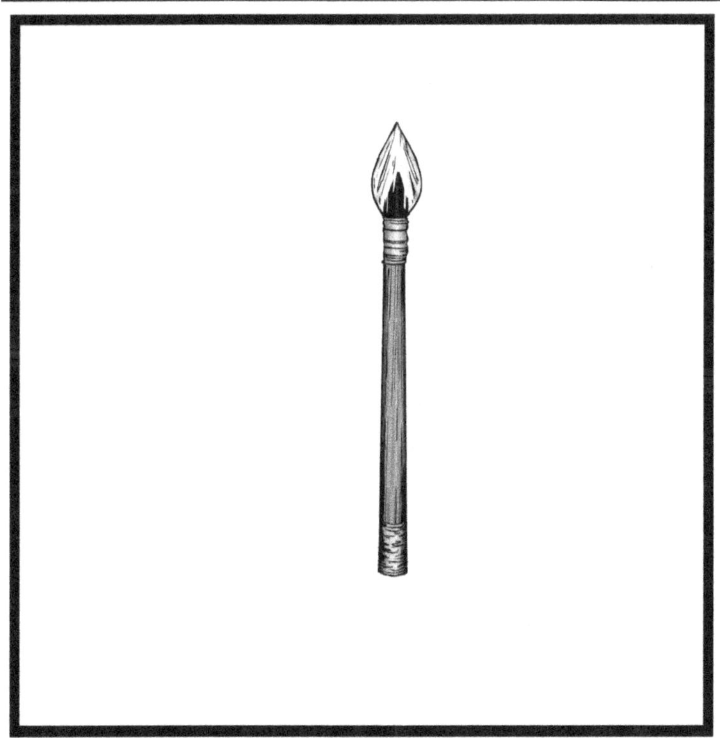

"What is the correlation here?" said Anthony. "The image pairs that you see appear to be somewhat random." Lucia replied, "Perhaps what's even more mysterious is how these images reveal themselves in the first place and only to Lucas."

"Do you see anything in the key now?" asked Nate.

Lucas reached into his pocket and took out the key. He examined it closely and said, "No, nothing now."

As he was about to put the key back into his pocket, his eye caught the key face. "Wait a minute, I think I see something now." He carefully inspected the key and rotated it slightly so that he could view it from different angles, then he replied, "Yes, there's something here. I see a peanut!"

"What?" said Anthony, "I've been wanting peanuts all morning long since the girls' game started. Do you see any crackerjacks?" Everyone laughed. Lucas turned the key over and saw the peanut become the body of an instrument. "It's a guitar," he exclaimed. A few seconds later, both the images were gone. "You see," he said, "sometimes the images are past, sometimes present, and at other times they peer into the future."

Nate had brought the arrowhead with him, which he found the day before. He had polished it up to showcase its natural beauty. He passed it around to the gang so that they could take another look at it.

Everyone admired the well-crafted arrowhead. Lucia re-marked, "This is beautiful. If you look closely, you can see a vein of red flint running through one side in the shape of the letter 'C'." Lucas said, "Let me see that." He got shivers down his spine studying the detail in the arrowhead.

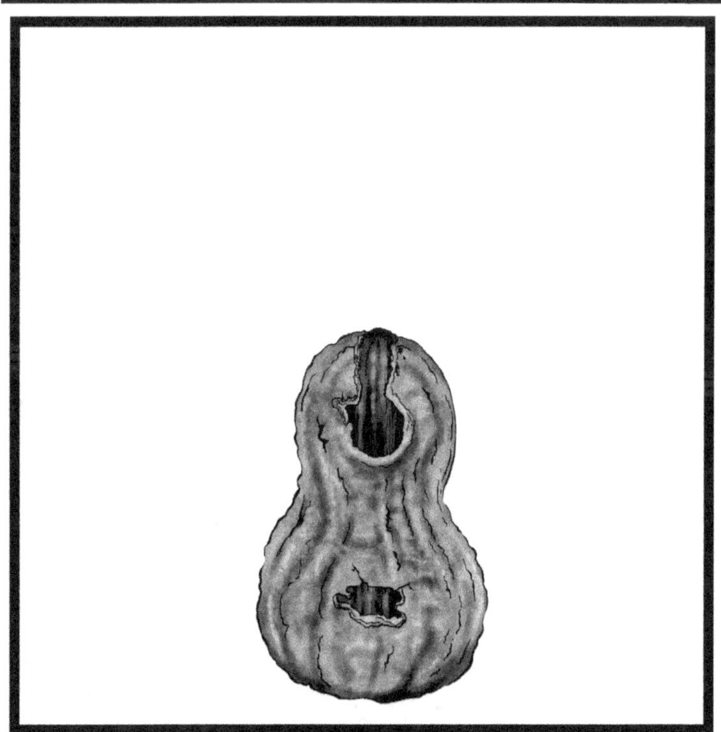

Pulling the key out of his pocket, he compared the new face side with that of the arrowhead. "They are indeed similar," he pointed out. "What's similar?" asked Kim.

"They both have the letter 'C' on their face."

Lucia responded, "A partial circle is a relatively common shape. The letter 'C' can be identified with any such marking. It is probably just a coincidence."

"Maybe," said Lucas, "and maybe not."

Nate added, "Either way, this arrowhead is truly a thing of beauty."

Just then, Kim's phone rang. The call was from Mr. Granzo. He wanted to know if the gang could come over and help him clear things out of his damaged restaurant that very day. Kim asked the others. Everyone was available, so she informed Mr. Granzo they'd come over that afternoon. The gang was happy to help Mr. Granzo and curious to see how much damage had been done to the pizzeria.

When they arrived, they found fallen chunks of stucco off the front of the building. Mr. Granzo, sweeping up some crumbled plaster and other debris off the floor, greeted them.

"Thank you for coming over on such short notice. I've been overwhelmed trying to clear this place out. Your help is very much appreciated." The gang jumped in and started boxing kitchen utensils that could be salvaged and used in the new Mustang Pizzeria. As they worked alongside Mr. Granzo, he talked of the many good days the gang spent at his place laughing and eating pizza together. He told his helpers there would be a special dinner for them after the new place was built and opened for business.

Next, he said, "Since I'm going to rebuild anyway, I'm thinking of expanding." Chelsea asked, "Do you mean that the new Mustang Pizzeria will be even bigger than this one?"

"Well, yes, it probably will be," said Mr. Granzo. "I am thinking even beyond that. I own the adjacent field, so perhaps I could build something new."

"Let me guess," said Anthony, "Are you considering building a bakery next door?"

"Bingo!" exclaimed Mr. Granzo. "How did you know that?" Thinking fast Lucia said, "Just the other day we were talking about how Sharefield doesn't have a nice bakery and that the town could use one."

Mr. Granzo replied, "That's amusing. Do you think it would do good business? I know a considerable number of Italian baked goods recipes." Kim answered, "If you are baking them, there's no doubt they'll be delicious."

After a couple of hours of intense work, the gang said goodbye to Mr. Granzo for the day and agreed to return and help again whenever he needed them. As soon as they left the premises, Dion said, "Enough is enough. We must start an all-out effort to discover what's going on with Lucas's key. This is all just too strange." Everyone agreed, especially Lucas, who had developed a burning desire to understand the key.

There were no questions about Lucas' visions anymore; everyone knew it was the key itself, revealing images only to him.

"This is quite a mystery. How does a key reveal so much and only to Lucas?" said Dion. Kim suggested, "We must follow every single lead we have. Remember, Victor told us that there could be another briefcase."

"Yes, but we already asked Claire and Daniel Martinez if they had seen anything in the mansion. We helped them clean it up after the old man's death a year ago, and they've been renting the rooms out since then. Mrs. Martinez told us that something as large as a briefcase would have shown up by now," said Chelsea.

"You are right, but we must probe every possible source of information to figure out why this key is so special," replied Dion.

"I will contact the Martinez's again and ask them if there's any way they could have somehow missed finding a briefcase anywhere in the mansion," said Kim.

"That is a good start," added Dion.

Lucas said, "I will go back to the Diyton hardware store where I had this key made and talk to George. Maybe he can offer some possible explanation for its strange behavior."

"Good thinking," said Chelsea. Nate offered, "We could give Victor another call to see if he has any more ideas."

"I think that would be wise," Lucas responded. "Remember, the key showed a computer mouse that became a carrier on top of a vehicle. Although I've never met Victor, I thought of him when I saw the image pair. He traveled across the country. Now we can contact him via a video conference on the computer."

"That's a great idea," said Nate. "It'd be good for all of us to be together and talk with him while we could see his smiling face."

"You could introduce me to him," said Lucas.

"You bet we will," said Kim.

10

INVESTIGATING THE KEY

The gang was now on an essential mission to unravel the mysteries surrounding Lucas's magical key. They planned on visiting the old mansion once again and talking with the employee at the hardware store where the key was made.

"There's got to be an explanation, and we're going to find it," said Kim.

"We've got a few good leads between us. Let's work together to make sure we cover all the bases," said Dion.

Lucas added, "I'll feel a lot better once we get to the bottom of this."

Nate responded, "Let's not forget Victor, our friend on the coast. When can we reach out to him? Lucas and I have soccer practice tomorrow morning."

"Maybe we can contact him after your practice," suggested Kim.

Lucia and Chelsea remained silent; they sat lost in their thoughts. The key was really bothering them. "This just doesn't add up," Lucia finally spoke.

Kim proposed that everyone gather in her basement after soccer practice the following day. She would set up her laptop so that Victor could join via video conference. Nate said that he would call Victor that evening to ensure that he would be available for the call.

At Kim's house the next day, the gang was eager to connect with Victor. Victor, equally excited, greeted them warmly through the screen.

After the hellos, Nate introduced Lucas to Victor. Victor said, "You look exactly as I pictured you."

"Wait a minute," Dion interjected, "How could you have formed any vision of Lucas?"

Victor replied, "Remember, I ordered a virtual reality system of my own after hearing of all your adventures. I set up my own world called *The Recovered View*. Knowing something about Lucas, I added him in, along with the rest of you. It just so happens that he looks quite similar in person."

Chelsea shivered. "That's a bit creepy, given our past virtual reality experiences."

Then Victor thanked the gang for sending him chocolates at a time when he really missed being with his old friends. Kim blurted out, "It was Lucas's idea, well sort of. He saw a chocolate kiss as the sail on a beautiful yacht."

"Well, okay," said Victor, "that explains everything," as everyone burst into laughter.

Then Lucia redirected the conversation, saying, "Let's get down to the business at hand." She asked Victor what he thought of their plan to contact Mr. and Mrs. Martinez. Victor nodded thoughtfully and said, "Well, you've already reached out to them once about the possibility of another briefcase. I doubt they'll have anything new to offer you. What you really need to do is to find a way to get back into the old mansion yourselves and search it, top to bottom. There may be clues in there that could lead to a second briefcase, even if you don't actually find one."

Kim's expression brightened. "That's a great idea, but the mansion is now a bed and breakfast. The owners live there on the lower level. It's unlikely we'll be able to search the place."

Victor paused, considering. "That may be true, but if you tell Claire Martinez that her sister has a similar key that would fit the same lock as the briefcase you're searching for, perhaps she'll find a way to accommodate you."

"Well, that's certainly worth a try," Lucia agreed. Lucas then shared with Victor how he had his key made at the hardware store in Diyton. He mentioned his plan to return and ask George, the employee who helped him, if any other strange incidents had been reported that were associated with that key-making machine.

Victor replied, "That's a promising idea. Ask him if anyone has reported a key that is out of the ordinary. Those types of machines are new, but as I think about it, all they do is grind brass key blanks into the shape of the one they are copying. It's not a likely lead, but worth a try."

"Yeah," Lucia chimed in, "how could a key-copying machine conjure up all sorts of relevant images that only Lucas can see?"

"You make a good point, but the key cutting is computer-controlled," said Anthony. "Cutting out a shape and creating images for Lucas are two entirely different things," replied Lucia.

"True," said Lucas, "but we don't have any other leads, and it's an easy stop for me to drop in and ask George if he has anything to add to our puzzle. Judging by the look he gave me when I asked him to copy a key for an unknown lock, he probably won't be too surprised."

Lucia replied, "When you talk to him, don't be specific. Just ask him if the machine has been acting funny and if anyone has reported any issues with the keys they had made from the machine."

Anthony looked straight at Lucia and said, "Yes, sometimes it is good to ask open questions. You never know how they will be answered."

"That's good advice," said Victor. "You don't want to tip your hand. Just ask him how the machine works."

With that, the conversation ended, and as they said their goodbyes, everyone agreed to stay in touch with Victor as they searched for a resolution to this convoluted mystery.

Lucia, Kim, and Anthony agreed to visit the old mansion the following day. As they swung the decorative patina knocker against the old wooden door, it made a solid thud, the vibration transferring into the weathered oak hardened by the decades. The massive door creaked open as Mr. Martinez slowly stuck his head out. He immediately broke into a gentle smile, recognizing the teens in front of him. Inviting them in, he asked how he could help them.

Lucia commented, "This place sure looks a lot better than the last time we were here." Much of the furniture appeared to be new yet appropriate for the era of the old mansion. Mr. Martinez remarked, "I see that you have an eye for such things." Then he added, "The ornate woodwork in this room still has a soft shine to it, displaying its natural beauty, thanks to all your hard work to clean it up."

Just then, Mrs. Martinez joined them in the entryway. She said, "Hello, my young friends." She was a kind lady; her laughter revealed her joy at seeing the gang that had helped restore the mansion last summer. Her presence immediately instilled a sense of comfort in the teens. They all exchanged greetings, and then Kim searched to find the right words. She began by asking, "How is this place doing as a bed and breakfast? I think travelers would be thrilled to spend a couple of nights here."

Mrs. Martinez thanked Kim for her question and replied, "We have been booked solid for the past several months and have full-capacity reservations over the entire summer." Lucia dropped her head, thinking, *How are we going to be able to get in if the mansion is booked for the entire summer?*

But Kim wasn't deterred. She quickly replied, "We are so happy for your successful business, but doesn't that mean that you never have a chance to take any time off for yourselves?"

"Funny that you should mention this," said Claire. "We do plan to shut the place down for a week and take a short vacation later this month. My sister is going to look after the place while we're gone."

"Oh, really," said Kim, her eyes lighting up with hope. "We have a special favor to ask of you. We found the previous owner's briefcase here last summer. We still believe that there could be another one somewhere. The mansion may provide us with clues to its whereabouts. Do you think we could have a look around while you're on vacation? The place will be empty at that time, after all."

Mrs. Martinez thought for a moment. "Well," she said, "I guess that would be all right. I seriously doubt you'll find anything here. We've been through every room numerous times, including the attic and the storage building off to the side of the house. If there were anything like what you speak of, we most certainly would have discovered it by now."

Kim replied, "Oh, thank you, Mrs. Martinez. We understand that it's unlikely, but we'd like to have a look just the same."

"I will tell my sister to leave the place open the morning you plan to be here. Just let me know what day you choose," said Claire with a smile.

"We'll do that. Thank you very much." As the girls and Anthony walked away, they couldn't contain their excitement at the opportunity to search through the old mansion once again, from top to bottom.

Meanwhile, Lucas stopped at the Diyton Hardware store after soccer practice that same week to talk to George about the key reproduction machine. As soon as Lucas entered the store, George recognized him, saying in a sarcastic tone, "Hello Lucas, I don't suppose you're here to make another reproduction of a key to an unknown lock, are you?"

Lucas felt a bit taken aback, but he sort of expected this type of reaction. "No," he said. Not wanting to describe what was happening with his magical key, he said, "I was wondering if you could tell me more about how this machine makes keys."

"There's not much to explain to you, my boy," said George, "as you saw when we made your key, you put in the original, and the machine scans it. Then it picks up the correct blank key shape and cuts a replica." He continued, "Usually, the customer brings the lock in with them and tries out the new key on the spot. We haven't had any returns of keys that did not work properly. Why does all this matter so much to you?"

Lucas had to think on his feet. He explained, "I've always been fascinated by the internal workings of machines and their control systems. I just wanted to see if there were any more details that you could share with me." It wasn't a complete fabrication. Lucas truly did have a passion for understanding how things worked. He loved to take apart and reassemble any old piece of hardware he got his hands on. His parents would save old, worn-out appliances just so he could tear them apart, down to the last nut and bolt, and try to reassemble them to their original condition or even improve upon them.

George replied, "Well, this is all the explanation I have for you."

Lucas thought that George's choice of words was a bit strange like he was hiding something. Then George added, "We don't much like making keys for unknown locks around here." Lucas realized that George was still suspicious of him, hence his subdued responses. It became apparent to Lucas that this was just another key-making machine with a scanner and a key-cutting mechanism. It wouldn't explain how he was seeing strange images in the key and how these images could relate to his and his friends' real lives. Even if there was some far-fetched explanation, he was not going to get anywhere with George. He thanked him for his time and walked out of the hardware store feeling like he might never uncover the truth behind the key's mystical powers.

The gang met in the park again and reported to each other what they had learned from their investigations. They decided to check out the mansion on the Wednesday of the week the Martinez's would be away on vacation. Kim said, "I'll inform Claire of our plan."

Later that evening, Chelsea realized she was missing one of her favorite earrings. She felt a pang of sadness, knowing that she had it on that afternoon in the park, where Lucia had complimented them. Chelsea thought to herself almost jokingly, *maybe Lucas will see my earring in his key and tell me where I lost it. I cannot imagine what happened to it.*

The gang gathered at Sharefield Park for Kim and Chelsea's softball game the following Saturday. Nate and Lucas had just finished their soccer practice before the game. The girls played great that day and won by three runs. Lucas and Nate's soccer team were enjoying a successful summer too, boasting a record of four wins and only one loss so far.

Amidst all the mystery surrounding the keys, the gang found solace in the familiarity of their summer sporting events. It allowed them to take their minds off all the strange happenings.

II

THE SEARCH

The day to search through the old mansion arrived quickly. Everyone met in the park that Wednesday morning before walking to the mansion on the edge of town together. As they strolled along, conversation buzzed about how Ms. Brock possessed a key identical to Lucas's. They wondered if they would find anything new, and if so, should they share their findings with Ms. Brock. After all, she remained unaware that it was Lucas who had stumbled upon her key and graciously returned it to her.

Upon arrival, Dion rapped on the door, but no one answered. With a cautious twist of the handle, he pushed the door open, revealing the inviting interior.

He remarked, "Wow, this place looks stunning. It is how I remember it, but all the furnishings the Martinezs have added really make the place look authentic. No wonder their business is booming."

Nate gestured towards the ornate crown molding that surrounded the room and described to Lucas how he and the gang spent days meticulously cleaning it, along with the rest of place, restoring the historic mansion to its former glory. Lucas said, "You did a remarkable job. Everything in here really complements the old place."

"Alright, let's get focused," Kim declared. "We must leave no stone unturned. Let's split into two groups to cover the entire place more efficiently." Lucas, Nate, Kim, and Anthony agreed to work downstairs while Lucia, Chelsea, and Dion started upstairs.

Kim added, "Now remember, our main objective is the briefcase, but keep an eye out for anything that could be opened with a key. Check every nook and cranny before moving on. Once we're done with the main floors, we can explore the attic and the storage buildings together."

"Yes, boss," said Dion before he and the others headed up the stairs. They started by stepping into one of the seven bedrooms. The three teens scoured the room, searching the closet, under the bed, and behind the big aquamarine Victorian chair that was laced with brass tacks, set in the corner of the room. Nothing looked unusual.

Chelsea turned her attention to the drawers of a carved antique dresser with a large, majestic mirror mounted on top.

It was positioned against the wall opposite the bed. She said to the others, "This is where guests stash their clothes, so, it's probably empty." She opened each drawer one by one to find them empty as expected until she reached the lower right-hand drawer. It stubbornly stuck halfway open. From what she could see inside, it appeared to be vacant as well. She decided to move on. The drawer did not look big enough to hold a briefcase anyway.

After checking all the drawers of the smaller dresser in the same room, Chelsea remembered Kim's instruction to leave no stone unturned. She decided to revisit the mirrored dresser and attempt to pry that drawer open. She pulled on it again, but she met the same resistance.

She called Dion over for assistance, who gave it a try. Gripping the drawer handle tightly with both hands, he positioned his foot against the base of the dresser and pulled as hard as he could. There was a loud, sudden pop. The drawer shot forward along its tracks, stopping abruptly as it reached its limit. The instant deceleration of the drawer caused Dion to lose his footing. He fell backwards onto the wooden floor. Lucia rushed over. Chelsea anxiously asked, "Are you alright?"

Dion, lying supine, looking up at her answered with a sheepish grin, "Hurt my pride, nothing more," as he sprang to his feet. Drawn by the commotion, the rest of the gang came running up the steps to see what was going on.

Dion peeked into the back of the open drawer, and his eyes widened as he caught sight of what appeared to be the short side of a briefcase. Just then, Lucas and Nate entered the room.

Dion announced, "Chelsea found a drawer that wouldn't budge, but we managed to open it. Take a look at the back. What do you see?"

Lucas peered into the drawer using the flashlight on his phone and said, "It looks like the side of a briefcase or maybe a small suitcase."

"Exactly," said Dion. "We need to get behind this dresser and investigate further." Nate and Lucas each got on one end of the dresser and tried to lift it. It proved too heavy for them to manage alone. The massive dresser had short legs that positioned the bottom drawers just a couple of inches off the floor. Dion thought for a moment and then asked, "Are there any canned goods in the pantry downstairs?" Kim ran down to check, unsure of Dion's plan but eager to assist. She was as excited as everyone else to see what was in that drawer.

She returned with two cans of squash soup, saying, "This is all that I could find." To which Dion replied with a smile, "We aren't here for lunch. Let's try to tip the front edge of the dresser up and roll these cans under it."

"Smart idea," remarked Anthony, "unless the weight of the dresser squashes the squash, putting us in hot water with cold squashed soup soaking the floor."

"I think the two cans together will support the weight of the dresser enough for us to roll it forward so that we can look behind it," proposed Dion optimistically.

"What if they aren't strong enough?" said Lucia. "Can't we use anything else to put under the dresser?" Kim suggested,

"I saw several small logs in the wood rack next to the fireplace downstairs." "That would certainly be safer," Anthony replied.

"We do not want to make a mess all over the floor," said Lucia.

"Let's check to see if the logs are the right size to work."

Kim and Lucia returned with several small logs – about the same diameter as the cans. They looked solid.

Dion said, "Great, we will use these."

Anthony added, "If Lucas and Nate can tip the front end up, Dion and I can roll the logs under the bottom front of the dresser." The mirror, mounted on the back of the dresser, made it a little easier to raise the front edge. Once the logs were in place, the four boys together lifted the back end of the dresser off the ground and pushed it forward. It rolled on the logs until the front legs came back down onto the area rug covering the hardwood flooring.

"That should be enough," huffed Dion as he slid in between the back of the dresser and the wall behind it. He noticed that the back panel of the dresser had pulled away, and a case of some sort was sticking out the back, trapped between the drawer it was in and that back panel. He maneuvered it out and held it up for everyone to see. "Look," he said, "here is our other briefcase!"

Kim exclaimed, "Why, this one looks just like the one we found before!"

"Only it's in much worse condition," Lucia pointed out. She continued, "This is strange. I wonder how long it has been trapped in that drawer. The top of the briefcase must have hit the inside wall of the dresser, preventing the drawer from opening. It could have been secured in that drawer for quite a while, especially given how hard it was for us to get it out."

"Speaking of getting it out, we need to repair this dresser and put it back in place before we go any further," said Dion. Everyone agreed.

Nate chimed in, "I bet that there's a hammer in the storage shed beside the mansion."

Chelsea and Anthony headed off to the shed to investigate. Sure enough, there they found a toolbox equipped with everything they needed to reattach the back panel to the dresser. The Martinezs kept the tools on the premises to make small repairs between customer stays. Dion took the hammer that Anthony handed him and tapped the back panel back into place, reinserting the nails into their original holes. Then, the gang repeated the process with the logs to maneuver the oversized dresser back into place against the wall.

"Well, we have what we came here for. What luck! Let's head back to the park and see if we can get it open," said Kim. Lucia took out her phone and said, "I'll text Mrs. Martinez's sister to let her know we found the briefcase and are leaving the old mansion so she can lock it up at her convenience." A quick response came back: "Where did you find it?" Lucia explained the entire story to Mrs. Martinez's sister in a lengthy text message.

The gang practically raced to Sharefield Park, excitement buzzing around them like bees. As Dion carried the briefcase, everyone's minds swirled with possibilities. Could it hold a computer? Or maybe a treasure of some sort.

"Why would the old man who lived in the mansion have two identical briefcases?" Kim pondered aloud. Though no one knew had an answer, they recalled Victor's words, suggesting there might very well be a second one.

Upon reaching their favorite oak tree in the park, the gang formed a tight circle, with Lucas and the mysterious briefcase in the center. Lucas carefully inserted his key into the lock, giving it a few wiggles until it slid into the lock. He tried to turn it, but the lock seemed stubborn. Everyone was disappointed.

Nate suggested, "Pull it out and insert it again. Maybe the lock has frozen up after sitting untouched for so many years." Undeterred, Lucas followed the advice, repeating the process until, finally, the key started to budge. He rotated it to the right, just a little, and then a minute inch more. At last, with a final gentle twist, the lid popped open. Everyone drew closer for a better look at what was inside as Lucas slowly raised the lid.

What they found was a little disappointing at first glance. A notebook, some loose papers, several pictures, and other assorted handwritten notes. Lucas plucked out a picture, his voice brimming with excitement to the point one could hardly make out his words, "That's my grandfather." He held it up.

Chelsea said, "Oh my, that's Fred when he was younger, but who's the man standing beside him?"

"Maybe it's the old man who owned the mansion. Perhaps they were pals," Dion suggested.

"There's an easy way we can find out," said Anthony. He pulled out his new phone, The Long Ranger Part Two, as he called it after his first one was waterlogged. He snapped a picture of the photograph, saying, "I'll send this over to Phillip. He knew the old mansion owner before his death. Maybe he'll recognize him in this photo."

"Good thinking," Lucia commented.

As Anthony fired off the text, Lucas picked up another photograph from the briefcase. It was another picture of his grandfather and the same mysterious man standing beside him, both clutching identical briefcases at their sides.

"I think we may have our answer already," Lucas remarked, holding up the picture."

The gang was amazed to see a younger Fred with a briefcase that matched the one sitting before them.

Just then, Anthony received a response from Phillip. It confirmed that the other man in the photo was likely a younger version of the old mansion owner. Another text followed, "Everyone called the old man Josh. "Anthony replayed to the gang, "Now we have confirmation that Fred and Josh knew each other."

Then Kim said, "What else is in the briefcase?"

Lucas retrieved a notebook bearing his grandfather's name and flipped it open. Inside were diagrams of football plays from Fred's days as a pro player. "Wow," Lucas breathed, "this is something I really want to keep."

He dug further into the case and discovered several notes to his grandmother from Fred, expressing his love for her. They were written during Fred's time in the service, before his professional career. As Lucas quietly read one of the letters, he mused, "It must have been even harder in those days to be away from family for so long. They didn't have all the communication channels we enjoy today. Their correspondence was limited to letters and maybe an occasional long-distance phone call, often with bad reception."

Nate nodded in agreement, "Yes, we chat with Victor all the time and just take it for granted."

Kim Asked, "Do you mind if I see one of the letters? I think it is so romantic that Fred would handwrite them."

Lucas said, "Sure," as he handed one of the notes to Kim.

Dion remarked, "Well, we all have a soft side. It is just not always apparent, especially to those we are most attracted to." Kim stopped reading for just an instant, looking up at Dion. Their eyes met, and then she quickly shifted her glance downward to the letter she was reading. She was touched by the letter and Dion's comment at the same time.

Lucas then pulled out a formal typed letter addressed to Joshua P. Coltrain. Fred's name wasn't on it. It was a letter of appreciation for Joshua's service, acknowledging his role as the team's head chef.

As Lucas read it aloud, Anthony exclaimed, "So Josh and Fred were both part of the same football organization and probably traveled together a lot."

Lucas added, "In those days, Josh probably wore several hats. The league wasn't as well-funded as it is today. We're talking pre-Super Bowl era."

"I wonder how Ms. Brock ended up with a key to this briefcase so long ago," said Chelsea.

"This briefcase is pretty beat up," observed Lucia, "maybe Fred just discarded it, or left it with Josh at the mansion way back then and never recovered it."

Lucas chimed in, "When my grandmother died, we were living out of town, but I remember my parents talking about how distraught Fred was. It wasn't much longer before he moved to the assisted living facility in Sharefield. It's possible that he left the briefcase with his friend Josh at the old mansion around that time. As for Ms. Brock's key, I have no idea."

"Maybe that's why Fred drew a key on the back of the note he left for us. Seeing Dion's key, he might have wanted to let us know he once had a similar one. Perhaps he remembered his old briefcase was with his friend Josh," Chelsea suggested.

"That makes some sense," agreed Kim.

Suddenly, it hit Lucas that he was holding an important piece of his family's history, and he wanted to share it with his parents. However, he and the gang had promised to keep the key secret as they tried to figure out why it had such special powers.

"I need to share this with my family," Lucas declared. "What if I tell them the story of finding Ms. Brock's key and making a copy and how it led us to this briefcase without mentioning that it somehow has powers beyond anything we can explain?"

Understanding the significance, everyone agreed that Lucas should share this history with his family. Nate raised a question, "Can you tell them about the briefcase without mentioning the key's special powers?"

Lucas chuckled, "They probably wouldn't believe me anyway. You had doubts about it yourself for some time."

"I guess that's true," Nate admitted.

"We still need to figure out why Lucas's key is so special," added Kim. "But we all agree that Lucas should share this briefcase with his family."

Dion helped Lucas strap the briefcase onto the back of his bike then he left for home to show his parents what he had found. Later that day, as Chelsea and Kim were on their way home, they stumbled upon a scraggly looking dog in distress. It was rummaging through trash, not having eaten anything in several days it seemed. Despite their attempts to call the dog, it remained preoccupied with finding food. Approaching the skittish animal cautiously, they saw the desperation in its eyes. It was a small brown and black dog with white on its chest, resembling a border collie mix. The dog was timid at first, but fortunately, Chelsea had some dog treats that she always carried in her purse for her beloved Grand Paw when they went on walks.

She pulled out the bag and set a treat on the ground. The four-legged creature approached slowly, staggering with malnutrition. It dropped its head and gobbled up the treat as soon as it was within reach. Chelsea set another treat down that was quickly taken, and then a third one. Taking a chance, she held one in her hand. The starving dog approached cautiously, then snatched the treat with a quick flip of its neck. One by one, Chelsea gave the dog all the treats she had. Then she slowly reached out her hand and gently patted its head.

"We must do something for him," she said to Kim. Kim agreed, "Unfortunately, my family is quite allergic to dogs, so I don't see how I can take him as much as I would like to."

Calm and unresisting, the dog allowed Chelsea to pick him up and carry him home. She kept him outside, away from Grand Paw, and fed him all that he could eat. The dog seemed to rejuvenate somewhat after eating. He began to move around Chelsea's yard, sensing the presence of another dog in the vicinity. For most of the remaining day, he rested quietly on her back patio.

As Lucas arrived home, he unstrapped the old, tattered briefcase from the back of his bike and carried it into the house. His dad was particularly moved as soon as he saw the briefcase. He asked Lucas, "Where did you get that? Lucas recounted the story to his parents. Lucas's dad said, "I remember that briefcase from my youth. My dad always carried it with him on the road when he was playing away games. He kept all his football notes and personal items in it."

"That's right," said Lucas, "and a lot of them are still here."

The family reminisced about old times as they looked through the contents of the briefcase. Lucas's dad remarked, "Your mother and I stayed in that very room where you found the briefcase in the old mansion when we returned to Sharefield for your grandfather's funeral. I remember trying to open that drawer in the lower right of the mirrored dresser and was frustrated when it stuck. To think that my father's things were inside that drawer all this time. It's certainly nice to have them now."

Lucas's dad explained that everyone associated with the team was given an identical briefcase. "Fred and Josh always traveled together. They were always getting their briefcases and keys mixed up. My dad had his key changed to an alternative design so that he could tell it apart from the others."

Then he turned to Lucas and said, "I have something for you as well. I was going to save it until the time was right. Perhaps this is that time, now that you have located this special briefcase. When your grandfather died, I went through all his things at the Sharefield assisted living facility. In the lower drawer of his nightstand, I found an old key. I recognized it as the key to his briefcase. It was quite worn, like the briefcase here itself, but it had a certain charm to it. It was the unique design that your grandfather had chosen for it. I thought at the time that this was something that you might like to have, but it looked quite old. I tried to clean it up with little success, so I took it to the Diyton hardware store to have a copy made. I decided that I would give you a shiny new copy, then I threw the old one away. Here is the copy I had made for you."

Lucas's dad opened his hand and revealed the shiny new key with a face on both sides that matched the new side of Lucas's special key. It was different from the original key that Ms. Brock had received as a child.

Lucas was overwhelmingly grateful. With wide eyes, he accepted the key from his father's outstretched hand and slid it into the briefcase. It turned the lock just like his special key had done.

Beaming, Lucas said, "Now I can understand how the key copying machine at the Diyton hardware store might have malfunctioned. It must have stored the key you copied in its memory, which was the same general shape as the key I had scanned from Ms. Brock. It's not hard to imagine that there could have been an error in the software, resulting in a hybrid key of the same shape but with one of each of the two faces. Especially since the key cuts, specific to the lock it opens, were exactly the same."

Lucas thanked his parents, emphasizing how having both keys made them even more special, serving as a reminder of his family and the love they shared.

Meanwhile, when Chelsea's dad returned home from work, she introduced him to her newfound friend. She was eager to keep him as she told her dad that he would make a great companion for Grand Paw. Chelsea's dad nodded, saying, "The first thing we need to do is to make a trip to the vet and have the little guy checked out." Chelsea agreed, and they made an appointment for the next day.

As Lucas prepared for bed that evening, he pulled out his special key to compare it once more with the new one his father had given him. Suddenly, a new image emerged from his two-sided key. It was a picture frame, quite like the frame around the mirror on top of the heavy dresser that he and his friends had moved earlier that day. Flipping the key, the frame transformed into a fireplace, just like the one in the lower level of the old mansion where Kim had discovered the logs used to move the dresser away from the wall. Lucas quickly grabbed the new key his father had given him, checking for any similar images on its face. There were none.

This left Lucas both upset and reassured. He was a bit unnerved by the mysterious images yet comforted by the certainty that there must be an explanation. Determined more than ever to uncover the truth, he set the key on his nightstand before drifting off to sleep. Just before closing his eyes, he checked his special key one last time.

A picture of a soda cracker appeared, prompting a chuckle as he turned it over and saw the cracker reveal a stamp on a letter akin to those found in the briefcase Fred had sent to his grandmother many years ago.

The following day, Chelsea and her dad took the malnourished dog to the vet for an examination. The fella looked better in the morning, although he was still quite weak. The vet administered his shots and advised Chelsea to feed him extra portions of food and keep him separated from Grand Paw until he regained his strength. Chelsea and her father were relieved to hear the news. Chelsea suggested they name him Bongo, noticing how he swung his front leg back and forth in rhythm whenever music played in the background.

Later that afternoon, Lucas shared with the gang what had transpired the previous evening. Lucia pondered, "So maybe we've figured this out. Since Fred had replaced his briefcase key with one that had his own design, he likely got rid of the original key that he was confusing with everyone else's key. His friend Josh, who's a distant relative of Ms. Brock, gave her the discarded key at a family reunion when she was a young girl. She held onto it all these years until she lost it that day at Diyton South Side, where Lucas found it."

"Things are finally starting to make sense, that's except for those strange images that keep appearing in Lucas's special key," Kim remarked.

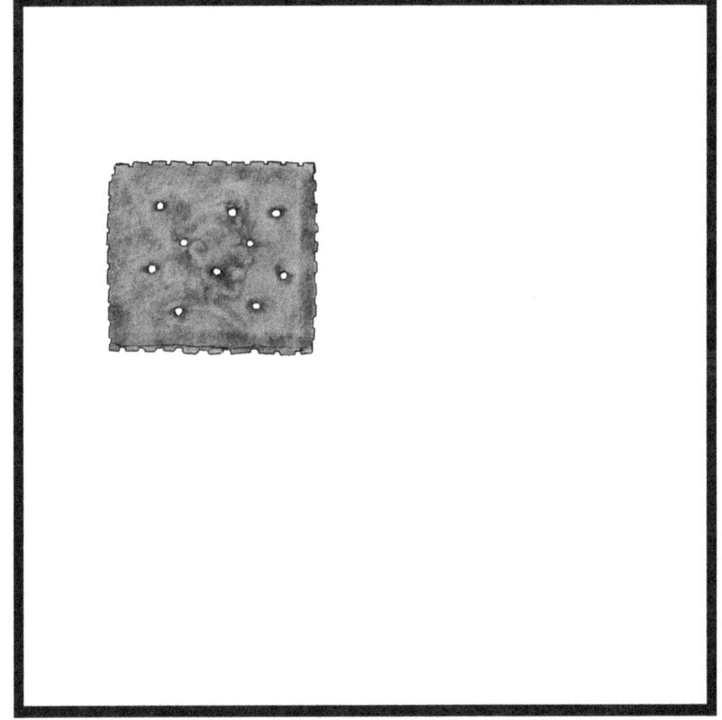

12

DIFFICULT DECISIONS

Mr. Granzo had asked the gang for one final favor: to assist him in salvaging the rest of what they could from his cherished Mustang Pizzeria before its demolition. Everyone in town was sad at its closure but enthusiastic about the brand-new restaurant and bakery that would replace it.

The gang met Lucas in Sharefield Park after his ride down from Diyton, and they all headed over to the pizzeria together. Along the way, they talked about how Mr. Granzo was going to have his hands full trying to manage a bakery along with his new restaurant.

"He will most certainly need some help," said Kim. "Maybe I will learn how to bake cakes and pies with him someday."

When they arrived, Mr. Granzo greeted them with a smile and asked them to work in the back room. A room which they had not seen on previous visits. It was filled with additional cooking utensils, pots and pans, and other supplies that could be recovered. Together, they loaded everything up on a big truck to be stored off-site until the new restaurant and bakery were ready.

This was the last day for Mr. Granzo at his old place. He had been making pizzas and other great Italian food there for the past twenty years. As he stood in front of the building, Kim took his picture then he turned around for one last look. A tear welled in his eye, a mix of sadness and joy. He knew that he had built something of value and had the support of the entire community, along with his special friends, the Sharefield Gang, as he would begin to rebuild.

Upon securing everything in the truck, he told the gang that he couldn't stay around for the demolition of the workplace he had called home for so long. He explained that he was headed to a convention with other restaurant owners where he could learn from others.

"All the restaurant owners will gather to talk about the ins and outs of managing their own place. We'll all share tips and tricks." The convention was to be held in a big city at a center directly across the street from a huge aquarium, which was quite an attraction. Mr. Granzo said, "I'm looking forward to visiting this exceptional aquarium. I'll probably stay an extra day after the conference just to explore all the marine life exhibited there. It'll remind me of my home, growing up along the coast of Italy."

Mr. Granzo was a renowned chef. Anthony said that he made the best pizza in the entire state. He had an impressive display of awards on the walls of his kitchen to prove it. They were all packed away, now waiting for the new place.

"I was invited to give the opening keynote presentation early the first morning of the conference. It'll be quite a formal affair with an open breakfast for all, including lots of fresh fruit and pastries." Mr. Granzo added in a rather joking voice, "I will probably pick up a few things for my bakery just from the breakfast spread."

Dion and Kim found that to be breathtaking. He was a man who led by example, and they respected that. Kim said, "Mr. Granzo, I wish that we could all be there to hear your speech. We know that you're about to leave, but would you mind rehearsing your speech with us? It'll mean a lot to us to hear what you'd share with the other chefs and restaurant owners."

Mr. Granzo was flattered. He said, "I'd be delighted to! A practice run will be a good rehearsal for the conference." He exited the truck and stood leaning against the rear of the truck. The gang gathered around and sat on the ground in front of him.

Mr. Granzo spoke in a settling voice that expressed confidence, sensitivity, and compassion. He talked of the importance of having a good plan that included contingencies for unknown setbacks. Then he turned and looked directly at each member of the gang as he spoke of the value of good employees and the mutual respect between the owner and its workers. He described the relationship as one of family. He went on to talk about the value of community, the restaurant services, and the importance of maintaining good relationships, even in tough times. Mr. Granzo eloquently reflected on the value of demanding work and the sustained effort required to build a successful business.

He said, "You have to have a strategic plan and stick to it the best you can while making adjustments as needed based on the circumstances." Finally, near the end of his speech, he said, "I'm going to give away the recipe for one of my most popular dishes to all attendees. I know that I'll benefit from the wisdom others share at the conference and want to do my part in adding value to the event." Then he thanked the gang for listening attentively.

The passion in his words moved everyone. As they stood up in silence, they embraced Mr. Granzo and wished him well on his journey.

Kim said, "You are going to have a profound impact at that conference. They'll all be so enriched by your words. We wish you the best." Mr. Granzo nodded his head as he got in the truck, then slowly drove away, glancing one last time at the Mustang.As the gang started their walk back to Sharefield Park, Lucas pulled his two-sided key out of his pocket. He saw a meat cleaver in the center. Flipping it over, it became a suitcase being pulled by a man.

"Well," he said, "I guess Mr. Granzo is on his way, as per my key."

"Let me see," said Chelsea. As per the ritual, the images just disappeared. Chelsea said, "Lucas, you may be seeing images in this key, but all I see is a pretty piece of metal."

"Yes, that's how it always goes," replied Lucas. Chelsea handed the key back to him, and they resumed strolling along. Chelsea remarked, "Lucas, you have many gifts that I admire. The images you see in this key are just one of them."

Nate commented, "Mr. Granzo will be in a different time zone when he gives that speech, and he is scheduled to present first thing in the morning. If it were me, I'd have difficulty adjusting to the time difference and making sure I was ready to present before a big crowd."

"Yes, he may not sleep well the night before," said Kim. "But I believe he will be on time and do a remarkable job because he really believes in what he's conveying to the audience. Did you see the look on his face, hear the passion in his voice?"

"I think we all did," said Dion.

Lucas was still holding his key in his hand, in which he was now looking at a pizza cutter that transformed into the pendulum on a clock.

"My key is listening to everything we're saying. The intelligence behind this is both astonishing and frightening at the same time."

"It's a bit creepy if you ask me," said Kim.

Lucas shook his head in agreement and said, "There is an explanation, and we shall find it."

Finally, at the park, they thought of Mr. Granzo and how fun it would be to travel to a big city and visit all the attractions, such as an aquarium teeming with sea life. Nate remarked, "Victor told us there are so many things to explore and learn from large cities like the one that he lives in now."

As Lucas jumped on his bike on his way home to Diyton, he basked in the sense of achievement after a day of adventure and purpose. That evening before bed he pulled the key from his pocket to set it on the nightstand. Once again, there was an image on the key. This time, it was a strawberry. He thought about breakfast at the conference Mr. Granzo was going to attend. As he turned the key over, he saw the strawberry become a stingray swimming around a coral reef. Despite his fatigue, Lucas found it difficult to sleep, believing that the key was somehow observing his every move, day and night.

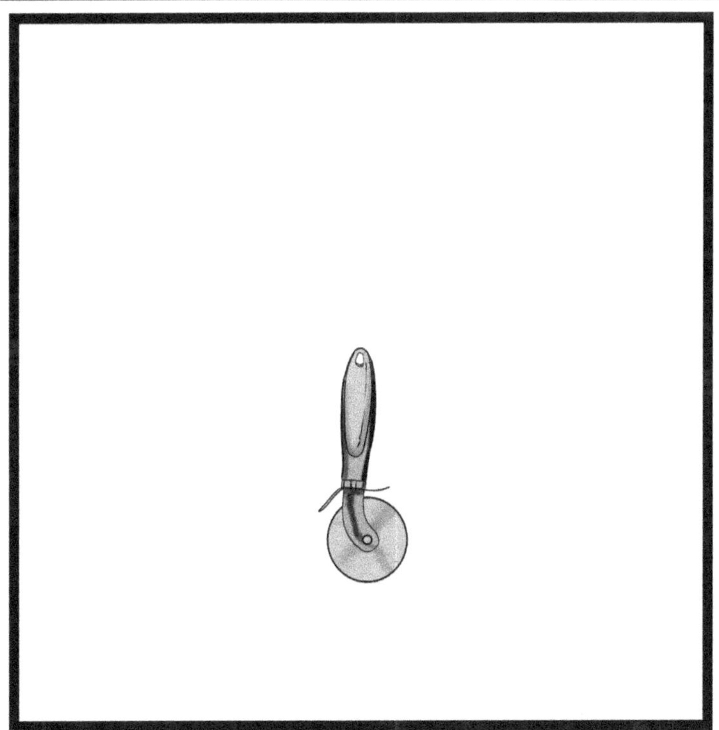

That same evening Lucia was making socks to give away as gifts. She enjoyed working with textiles whenever she had free time; it helped her relax and unwind after a busy day. Her mind drifted off into a daydream. She envisioned herself several years older, an accomplished interior decorator sought after by numerous clients. She imagined herself jet-setting to bustling cities like Mr. Granzo had described. Lucia knew she wanted to do something that combined her passion for artistic expression with a practical and useful profession. Of course, she realized there was plenty of time to discover and to consider the possibilities. She had to be open to and conscious of the opportunities while working toward more immediate goals at hand. Everything was bound to come together, even if her longer-term destiny wasn't clear at this juncture.

The following day, the Sharefield select soccer team had a rare home game at the park. The gang showed up for the excitement and to support Nate, Lucas, and the rest of the team. It turned out to be a thrilling game. The Sharefield team won by a score of four to three, with a goal in the final seconds. It was a headed pass from Nate to Lucas, who drilled the ball around his defender into the upper right corner of the goal. The opposing goalie lunged for the ball and managed to tip it as it flew past him into the net, sealing the win for the Sharefield Select team. Everyone cheered as the boys walked off the field in victory.

The gang settled under their favorite oak tree afterward. Nate and Lucas were still drinking water, trying to hydrate after a grueling game in the morning sun. A celebratory mood was in the air, with a hometown victory in hand.

After enthusiastic chatter, recapping the highlight of the game, the conversation turned to the evening before. Lucas described seeing a strawberry in the key before bed transform into a stingray swimming around a coral reef. Dion said, "Mr. Granzo has really made an impression on your key, Lucas." Everyone laughed, but the harsh reality was that it was true, and no one could explain how these images kept appearing repeatedly.

To take everyone's mind off the dilemma that would obviously not be resolved so soon, Lucia shared her thoughts from the previous evening. She explained to the gang how she was excited about future possibilities and simultaneously intimidated by the unknown. "It's just like Lucas's key," she said. "It's wonderful to have so many gifts and opportunities for growth, and at the same time, it's scary to have so many unknowns." Nate said, "The important operative here is time. Direction becomes clearer with time as we obtain more information. Things start to happen that influence us. A little fear is a springboard. It shoves us into action, keeping us focused on the objective."

"That may be true," said Lucia, "but that does not resolve my predicament right here at this moment. Sometimes, it creates a bit of anxiety just thinking about it." Everyone in the gang resonated with the sentiment, nodding in agreement. Deep down, they also knew that Nate was spot on about the process of unfolding knowledge over time. Nate summed things up saying, "I guess that growth comes with both discovery and challenge."

Lucas pulled the key out once again, feeling a hunch that it might have something to show him. He was right. The first image he saw was of a bottle cap. He recalled hearing about the gang's field trip to the design studio. As he turned the key over, the bottle cap became an area rug in a living room.

He described the images to the gang. Anthony said, "Lucia, maybe the key is saying that you should consider interior design."

"Maybe it is," replied Lucia. "I wish that such profound decisions could be that simple. It would be so nice if we could find an image in a key to help us make good decisions for our future."

Lucas said, "Perhaps different people see things in different ways. Figuratively, the answer may not just appear in the center of a key for everyone."

"It seems to work for you, my friend," said Nate. To which Dion replied, "I would like to ask your 'Jeanie in a bottle' key a few questions of my own." Everyone chuckled.

Lucas examined the key again, noticing a new image this time. "Hold up," he said, "now I see a sock." He turned the key over and watched the sock become a boomerang. He hesitated for a second as he contemplated the meaning behind this.

As Lucas explained to everyone what he had just seen, Chelsea added, "So much for always finding definitive answers to such puzzling questions from a key. One could interpret the boomerang as a change of mind toward or away from a decision."

"Yes, maybe, just maybe," Lucia pondered. "And maybe not," interjected Anthony as he smiled at Lucia. We agree the key is magical, but that does not mean it's always right, or that it knows everything," said Lucas.

"It may have had its foot in its mouth this time," said Anthony.

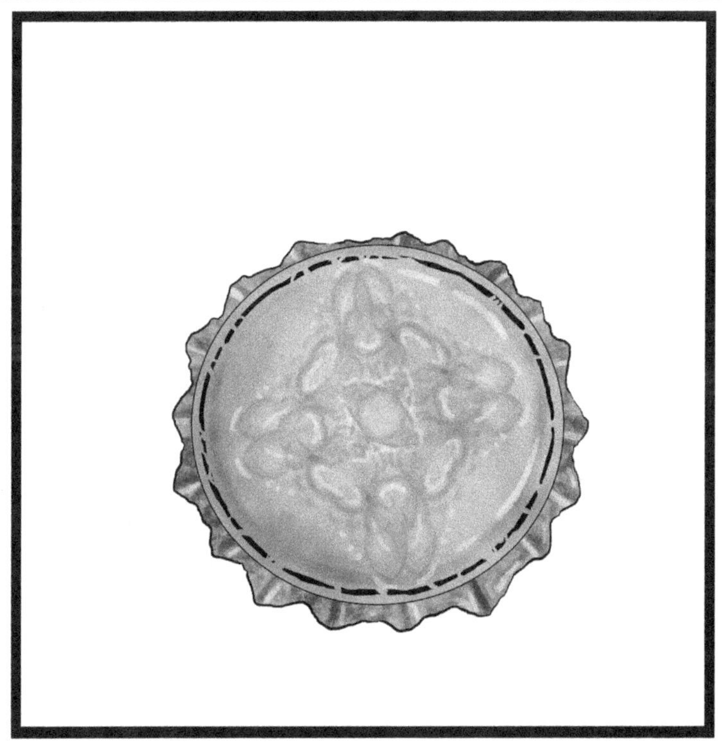

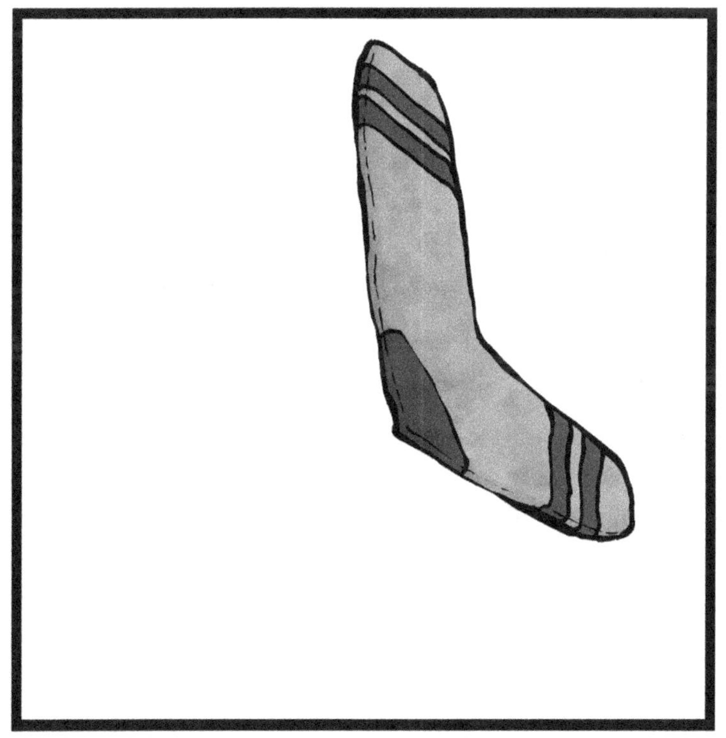

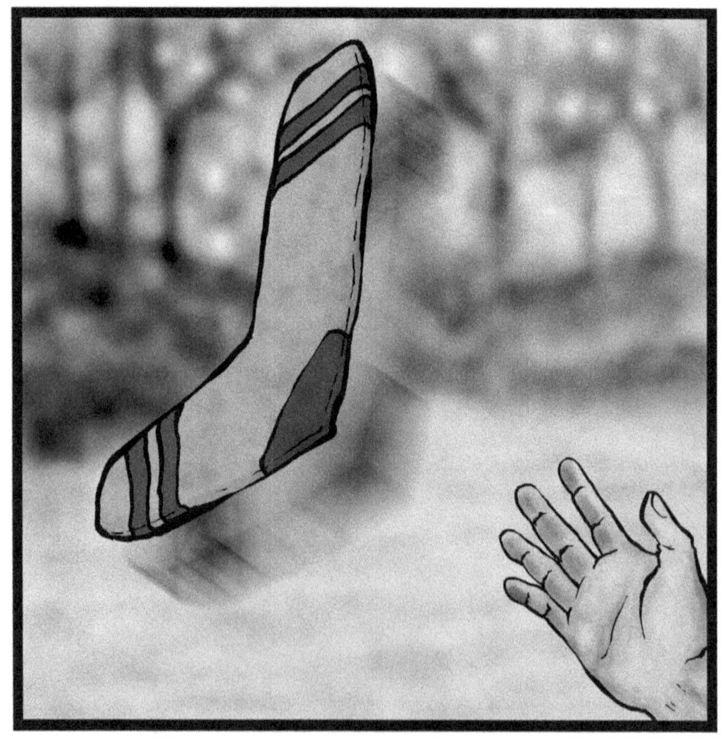

13

ONE TOO MANY
STRANGE CLUES

A couple days later, the gang met up in Sharefield Park again after soccer practice. Chelsea arrived after working out lifting weights at the gym. She told the gang about her new pet Bongo and showed everyone a picture of him. Lucia chirped, "We're happy for you. When can we meet this cute little guy."

"As soon as he's strong enough to get around," Chelsea responded. Kim remarked, "I'm pleasantly surprised that he's recovering so quickly. I was quite worried about him when we found him last week."

Then Lucas retrieved the shiny new key he had received from his dad and described in more detail what had happened when he took the briefcase home the other day. The gang was relieved to finally understand how the double-sided key was manufactured from the key-copying machine.

"A piece of the puzzle has clicked into place," said Dion.

"Yes," agreed Anthony, "but we still have no idea why or how Lucas is seeing transforming images in the two faces of his key."

"Do you ever see anything in the new key your father gave you?" asked Nate.

"Nothing at all," replied Lucas.

He pulled the two-faced key out of his pocket and said, "I did see several visions in this key the night we found the briefcase. I saw a mirror, which became a fireplace."

Lucia replied, "That must have been the mirror on the dresser where we found the suitcase back at the mansion."

"Exactly," said Lucas, "that's what I thought as well. I also saw a soda cracker become a postage stamp reminiscent of the letters my grandfather wrote to grandma." As he stared at the key, he exclaimed, "Oh wait a minute, I'm seeing something else in it right now. It's an earring." As he turned the key over, it became a swing on a tree.

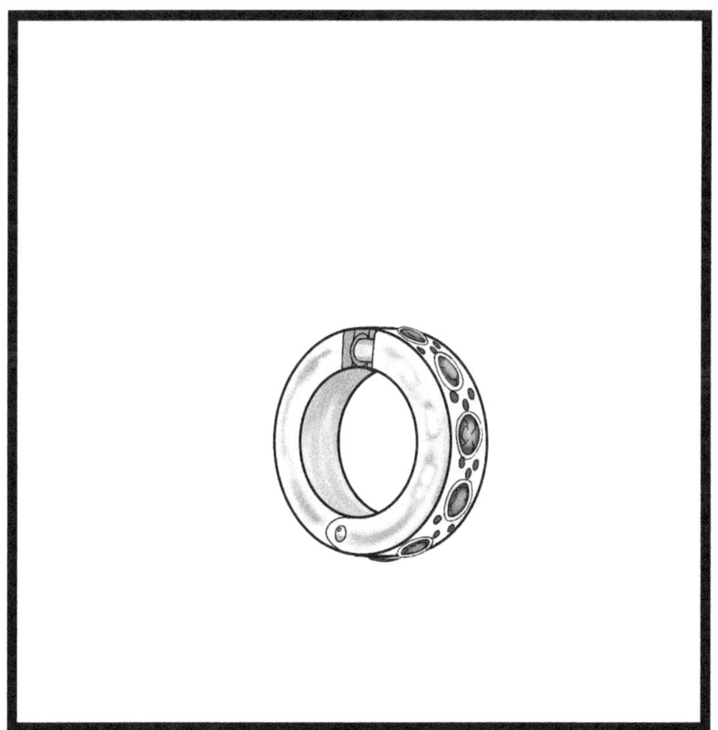

"Quick," said Chelsea, "let me see it," but the image vanished like before. She handed the key back to Lucas, looking rather disappointed. Then she thought out loud, "The image is gone, but maybe my earring is right under this tree where we always meet? We were here the day I lost it."

"Good point," said Anthony. "A ring under a tree is worth two lost in a bush."

Everyone began scouring the ground, kicking the grass in search of Chelsea's earring. Sunlight filtered through the large tree leaves speckled the ground. The shadows danced in waves, in response to the light breeze that oscillated the leaves. In one of the gyrating light patches, buried within the grass canopy, a pinpoint light intermittently flickered. It was as visible as the north star in the dark sky.

Chelsea saw it first and reached down to retrieve the very earring she had lost a couple of days before.

"Amazing!" she said as she held it up for all to see.

Anthony chimed in, "This feels too surreal. Let me see that earring. A dangling earring tree swing, go figure."

"Well, I was hoping that Lucas's key would help me find it," admitted Chelsea.

Lucas explained, "The mystical key is showing more as we speak. I'm seeing a weight in the shape of a dumbbell. On the flip side, it has become a toy bone in the mouth of a dog. Perhaps like Chelsea's new dog."

Lucas thrust the key toward Chelsea and asked, "Does this dog look like Bongo?"

Chelsea looked closely and replied, "Sorry, I don't see anything, but food has weighed heavily on Bongo's mind ever since Kim and I found him."

Lucas remarked, "This appears to be one of those periods when my key is very active." Before returning the key to his pocket he checked it one last time. "Just as I thought," he exclaimed, "now I see a tape measure, like one that would be associated with heavy construction. The back side of the key is showing me a large wrecking ball attached with a cable to a crane towering high into the air."

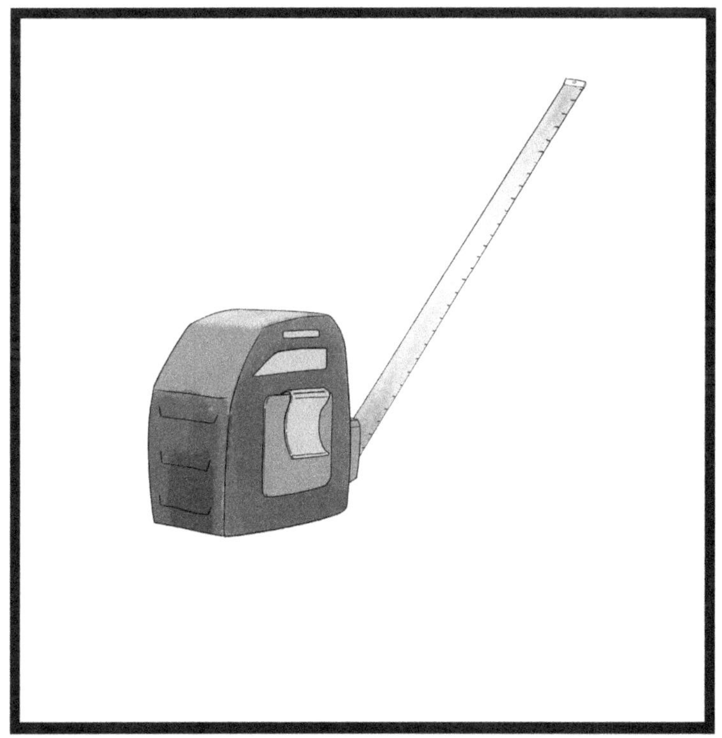

Dion reminded, "The demolition of the earthquake-damaged Mustang Pizzeria is scheduled for later this week." The gang had mixed feelings about watching the old building come down.

Kim added, "On the one hand, it'll be sad to see it go. On the other hand, it would be something interesting to see. We'll get the chance to bond with other townspeople in our community. Maybe some of our classmates will be there."

Anthony suggested, "I think this is something we don't want to miss. We might regret it later."

Lucia added, "Besides, we'll be able to relay to Mr. Granzo how the whole thing went. He didn't want to watch his restaurant being torn down in person, but I'm most certain he would appreciate hearing our account of the demolition."

Anthony said, "That is very thoughtful. You are always thinking of others."

Lucia replied, "Some people more than others," as she smiled back at Anthony.

Kim agreed, saying, "We should all be there."

Lucas joined the rest of the gang to watch the demolition. Upon their arrival at the site, they ran into Mr. Tortosa. He told them that after financing the repair of the Sharefield water infrastructure project, he wanted to make sure that the new Mustang Pizzeria, as well as the other businesses and homes in that part of town, always had a reserve of fresh water.

He had been discussing the construction of an additional water tower in the vicinity of the new pizzeria and bakery with the city management. Mr. Tortosa said, "It's exciting to see this area grow so rapidly. A new road is under development to access the water tower and surrounding businesses. The increased water service capacity will fuel further growth."

"All of you young adults have been a part of this progress. Mr. Granzo told me you've been a tremendous help to him in recovering his supplies from the pizzeria. You know, he and I go back a long way. I remember when he first considered building the Mustang. It was nice of you to help him out. I have complimentary tickets to our local festival for all of you. Maybe you've already heard about the festival. It's to take place later this summer. Thank you for supporting my friend and our community."

Kim replied, "It was our pleasure to help Mr. Granzo. The festival will be entertaining for all of us. Thank you."

The demolition of the city landmark was starting. A large crane with a wrecking ball on the end of a cable extending from the towering crane had arrived in town and set up the previous day. The operator stepped into the cab and began manipulating the controls. The ball swung from side to side like a pendulum on a clock out of time, inching ever closer to the side of the pizzeria. Then, with one swift motion, the cab swung around toward the building, like the head of a tiger searching for prey, bringing with it the massive arm of the crane from upward in the sunlit sky.

The swinging ball accelerated on its downward stroke and came crashing into the side of the Pizzeria like a freight train at full speed loaded with iron ore. The rumbling sound of the impact echoed throughout the town, followed by the crackling noises of falling bricks. The very wall Anthony used to lean against while sitting on the end table inside the restaurant came tumbling toward Mother Earth. It was as if gravity somehow multiplied right over the impact zone, drawing every loose piece of brick, stucco, and assorted construction materials to the ground in an accelerated instant.

A tear came to the eyes of the gang, and other members of the town as well. They painstakingly watched the crane destroy the rest of their favorite restaurant, one wall at a time. The place they had once spent so many hours laughing and eating with friends was just reduced to a pile of rubble before them.

When it was over, Dion was the one to break the silence, "I have so many fond memories of that place that will remain with me as I anticipate new experiences at the rebuilt Mustang Pizzeria."

"That's for sure," said Kim, giving him a side hug, "the best is yet to come."

Later in the evening, after dinner, Lucas was sitting on his front porch. He took out his key and saw an image of a road cone in its center. He flipped the key over to see it become the hat of a clown. He laughed as he put the key back in his pocket, making a mental note to tell his family about the festival in Sharefield coming up later that summer.

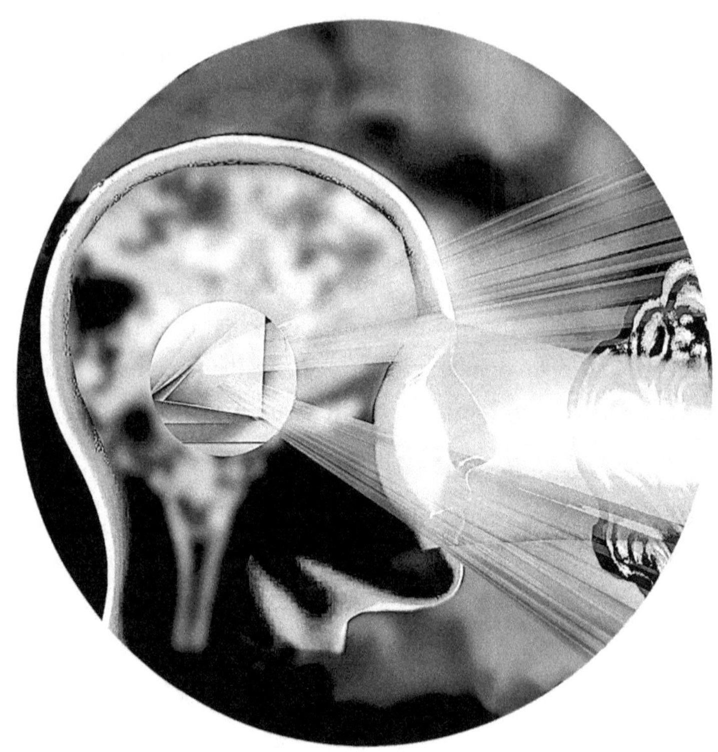

REFLECTION

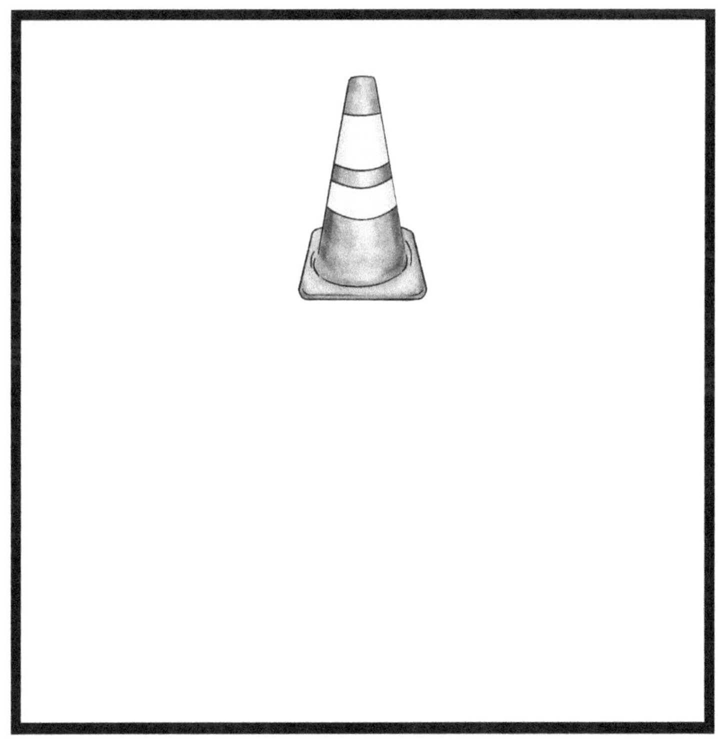

That night, Lucas had another strange dream. He was performing in a band at a formal social event. There was a fountain of fruit punch in the center of the hall, along with oeuvres and finger sandwiches. He strummed the guitar like a real professional. The band was playing old-time favorites for a mature crowd, and they sounded fantastic. In between songs, Lucas was asked to make some announcements and to introduce the other band members. The band included a great female singer named Chelsea, who was playing the tambourine.

Lucas awoke in a panic. His mother came running in, informing him that he was talking in his sleep and asked him if he was okay.

Lucas rubbed his face and said, "It was just a dream, a very strange one. I'm fine." Then he rolled over and drifted back to sleep.

The following day, he told Nate about his dream and they both laughed together. Nate replied, "I don't know which part is the funniest, you acting as the MC at a gala affair or Chelsea singing old songs. She has a rather contemporary taste in music."

Lucas agreed, saying, "Yes, it was a strange one, alright."

The team soccer practice was rained out that day. It started pouring about a half hour after the boys took the field. Chelsea and Lucia had come to watch the practice, accompanied by their umbrellas. It was a violent thunderstorm with lightning that lit up the otherwise dull gray surroundings like a strobe light at a disco dance. They all walked quickly over to Kim's house through the mounting puddles at every crosswalk.

After they arrived and dried off with fresh towels that Kim's mom had offered, Nate said to Lucas, "Tell Chelsea about the dream you had last night."

Lucas had pulled his two-sided key out of his pocket, which he habitually checked multiple times each day. As he started narrating his dream, he observed the key display an image of a microphone, which he quickly flipped over to find the microphone become part of a fountain with water spewing out of it.

He exclaimed with glee, "There's water coming out of a microphone!" A few seconds later, the images were gone. Lucas, still excited, went on to tell the girls about the rest of his dream in what sounded like one long, run-on sentence.

Chelsea replied, "Did you give a watered-down speech?" They all laughed at the absurdity of the dream. But just then, Lucas saw a light bulb in the key that became an image of the new water tower that Mr. Tortosa spoke of.

"My key is active again." Saying that, Lucas flipped it back to the first side and saw a thumbtack in the center of his key. As he turned it over again, this time it became an umbrella sheltering a woman underneath it.

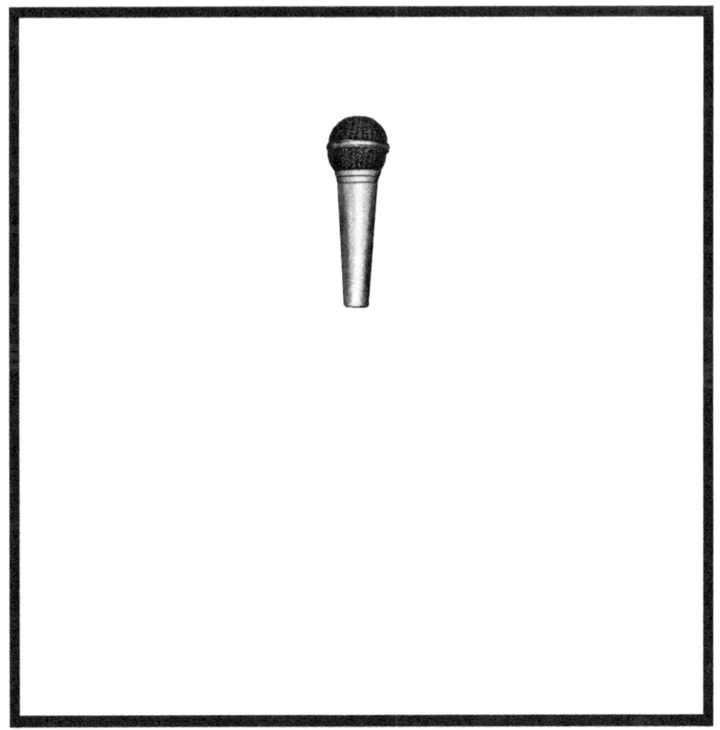

Lucas said, "These sets of images are related. They all reference water. I feel like they're trying to tell us something, in fact, I'm certain of it. Based on what we've seen in the past, the images from my key are relevant to our lives in some way." The others all agreed but no one had any insight as to their significance.

The rain had stopped. It was time for Lucas to return to Diyton. As he walked back to Sharefield Park to get his bike, he was thinking of the latest images that sprang forth from his key. The bike trail home was still wet. Cracks had developed in the blacktop after the earthquake, so he took it easy on the ride home.

He couldn't stop thinking about the significance of the last few images. He was concentrating so hard that he almost fell, having absent-mindedly ridden over breaks in the asphalt. He said to himself aloud, "These cracks in the pavement really need to get fixed." Soon after, he was home and ready for dinner.

Nate was equally bothered by the latest key images. He sent a text to Victor that afternoon asking him if he had any ideas about what they might mean. Unfortunately, Victor had no clue either.

That evening, Lucas saw on the news that there was a terrible outbreak of a virus in the big city of Shellington. Many people had been hospitalized, and there was concern all around that the virus might spread to the other outlying cities and towns.

Before hitting the hay that evening, he pulled out his key once again and took a quick look. He saw a bolt of lightning in the key that looked quite intimidating. He turned the key over to see the lightning become a crack in the blacktop on a track like the bike trail to Sharefield that he was now so accustomed to.

He fell asleep deeply, puzzled by all the water-related images.

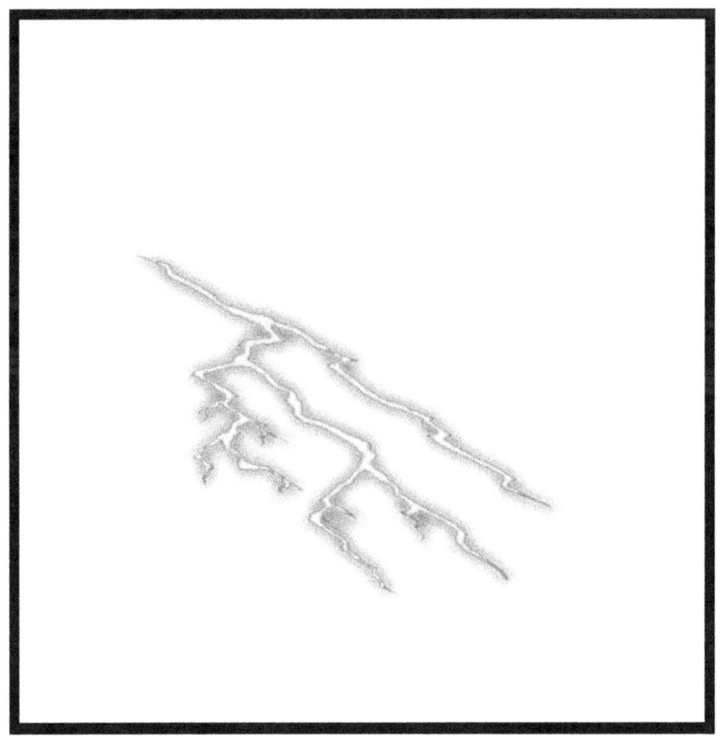

The next day Lucas and the Sharefield Gang gathered in the park after watching Kim and Chelsea's intense baseball game with a rival team. Despite a narrow loss by one run, the girls played with passion against the top-ranked team. Lucas was only partially focused on the game, his mind consumed by thoughts of his mysterious key. Once everyone had settled under their favorite oak tree after the game, he spoke up, "This is serious! We must figure out the message behind this latest set of key images. These clues having something to do with water, are all trying to tell us something important."

"Maybe you are overreacting," said Dion, "perhaps they're related to the new water tower that's going in near the new Mustang Pizzeria and the bakery. Mr. Tortosa has been on the news lately describing all the activity surrounding that project."

Lucas replied, "I don't think so. The images I saw last night were wisecracks with special meaning, and that's no joke."

"Speaking of news," Lucas added, "Did you hear about the virus that's infecting people in the city of Shellington?" Most of the others had heard the news.

"It sounds terrible," Chelsea mourned. "The hospitals are nearly filled to capacity."

"Let's all remain vigilant of any new developments," said Lucia. "Hopefully, it won't spread to other places."

Lucas pulled out his key and saw a syringe in the center of it. To his surprise, it became a high-rise building in a city on the flip side. "That virus is serious," he interjected, "the key is telling us that shots are involved."

Dion said, "I have heard that a new vaccine is being developed. What an admirable way to serve others in the science of medicine." Everyone reflected for a moment on the potential impact of such a virus if it were to spread and the immeasurable value of something that could curtail its onslaught.

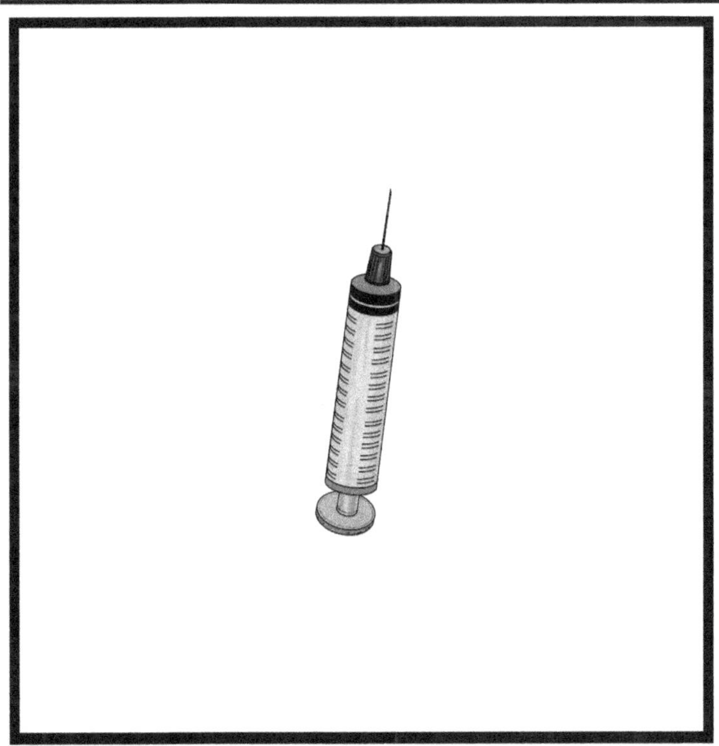

Then Kim broke the silence, "This latest set of images is further proof that Lucas's key has powers beyond what we could have imagined. Even though none of us can see what Lucas sees in that key, we need to consider his sightings very seriously."

Anthony replied, "So, regarding all the water-related images that Lucas has seen, what could possibly be their significance to us?"

Lucia said, "That's what we need to solve. How do they all relate to each other?"

"Well," said Chelsea, "the crack in the asphalt might somehow be tied to the earthquake, but that does not relate to water?"

"Or does it?" pondered Lucia. "Is there any way a thumbtack transformed into an umbrella can be coupled to a crack in the asphalt?"

Nate had an idea. "Let's get Victor on the phone and see if he has any insights. I already sent him a text about the water-related image pairs last night."

Nate called Victor and explained their dilemma.

Victor replied, "I understand the situation, but I just cannot put my thumb on a correlation that makes any sense."

Lucia rubbed her chin and replied, "Maybe you just did. You don't put your thumb on it. Instead, you put your thumb in it! Do you remember the old story we all heard as children?

A Dutch boy put his finger in the dike to save Holland? The saying, 'to put a finger in a dike,' means to delay impending disaster."

"Where are you going with all of this?" asked Lucas, curious.

"I'm not sure, but there's a relationship here."

Chelsea remarked, "Maybe the crack in the asphalt is a crack in a dam."

Dion replied, "Could it be the dam that holds and regulates the water of Lake Moon Glow?"

"So maybe the earthquake cracked the dam!" exclaimed Nate. "If it breaks, half of Sharefield will be flooded! This is serious. We must get this out to everyone."

Dion replied, "We can't just tell people that Lucas saw some images in a key, so we think Sharefield might be in danger."

"You make a good point," said Kim. Then Victor's voice came clamoring through Nate's phone, "It's not out of the question to suggest to Mr. Tortosa that the earthquake may have potentially caused some damage to the dam. Why don't you go there and have a look around? You might see something, and even if you don't, you can tell him that you were there and raise the question of the dam's integrity."

"That's a great idea," Kim clapped. "Let's head over to Lake Moon Glow tomorrow. Besides," she said, "with all the rain we've had lately, I bet the falls from the Wondering River that feeds the lake look magnificent."

14

DISASTER IN THE MAKING

The Sharefield Gang, along with Lucas, met in the park the next day after soccer practice. Lucas's mom had dropped him off and agreed to take everyone to Lake Moon Glow for the day. She carried a delightful book with her and planned to sit at a picnic table and read in the peaceful beauty of nature while the teens spent the day exploring the lake.

As Kim had predicted, the water in the lake was exceedingly high. It was overflowing into the tall grass that bordered the lake. The group had decided to hike up to the falls later in the afternoon. Their first order of business was to assess the dam for any potential danger or anything suspicious.

As they approached the dam, Nate said, "We really have no idea what we're looking for here, but I guess that we've got nothing to lose." As they stood on a hill at one end of the dam and overlooked the vast lake, sparkling with every ripple that reflected the bright sun, they noticed that the water was close, too close to the top of the dam. An occasional wave splashed over the top of the embankment and rolled down the opposite side, leaving a darker, wet trail that contrasted against the paper-white concrete wall.

"That does not look right," exclaimed Chelsea.

"This alone is enough to alert Mr. Tortosa. We're no experts, but it's easy to see that the lake water is clear up to the top of the dam," explained Lucia. "That should be enough for concern."

"We will likely see him later this week at the Sharefield festival," Kim pointed out.

After a picnic lunch, the gang enjoyed a leisurely hike adjacent to Wandering River up to the falls. Along the way, Lucia glanced at something strange on the trail just in front of her that quickly scurried off into the woods.

She yelled, "What was that?" Others caught a glimpse of it just as it darted out of sight. Anthony suggested that it looked like a rodent with a bad case of the pricklies.

"I think it was a porcupine," said Lucia.

Anthony, in a puzzled voice, replied, "I don't think I've ever seen a porcupine."

Lucia added, "They're not at all common in this area. Recent shifts in weather patterns over the past couple of years are causing all sorts of changes in animal migration that are most unpredictable."

By that time, Dion had looked up a picture of the porcupine on his phone. "That's what it was, alright, look at the picture."

Approaching the falls, they could hear the deafening roar of the rushing water. The gang rounded the bend in the trail as the falls presented themselves in all their glory. They were as enchanting as Kim had hoped they would be. Immediately, a gentle shower of mist greeted the gang, rising above the cascading water as it splashed against the rocks below. The gang took a seat next to the falls and reminisced about their past class pictures behind the falls and the key that Dion found there a year ago.

As they sat admiring the rainbow that appeared in the misty air, Anthony pulled a harmonica out of his pocket and began to play. No one even knew that he had one. He had been practicing privately at home until he was good enough to play several songs. Everyone was amused and delighted to hear the music, especially coupled with the beautiful setting. They all began to sing, making up lyrics as they went along and laughing at their own silliness.

Afterwards, they hiked to the bridge over the river to show Lucas the strange rock formation under the bridge that they had discovered on a previous visit. Lucas agreed it looked like a menacing prehistoric dragon. As Nate leaned over the bridge guard rail, he pointed to the features of the rock.

"See," he said, "there are the eyes and the mouth." As he did, the arrowhead which he had found at the Sharefield barbecue rolled out of his shirt pocket. It fell over the bridge and struck the strange rock formation. It threw off an electrifying continuous succession of sparks as the tumbling artifact bounced twice on the mysterious rock before falling into the river below.

"Oh no," bellowed Nate, "there goes my Indian-crafted arrowhead!"

"We must try to recover it," Kim said, sensing Nate's worry. "Maybe we can get close enough to the water to where it entered and find something to scoop it up."

"No," said Nate, "perhaps it is where it belongs now. The Indians had a deep admiration and respect for all of nature. The ground was sacred to them. They were, in effect, the first conservationists. We've just returned a part of their history to its rightful place among the rest of the rocks of the riverbed. I'm sad to see it go but honored to have held it for a while."

To this, Lucas replied, "Well, it did make a fire-breathing dragon out of that rock formation. That was a breathtaking and dramatic display."

The remainder of that glorious day was satisfying for all. The gang felt as though they were somehow in synchronization with the vibratory wavelengths of nature all around them. Lucas equated the feeling to the resonance he felt with his key when he hit the ground that day at soccer practice.

Later that week, the gang traveled together to the Sharefield Festival. Mr. Tortosa was taking tickets at the admission gate.

When the gang arrived, he teased, "Do you have legitimate tickets to come in here? These look fake to me."

Anthony retorted with sarcasm in his voice, "We don't know. We picked them up from a shady-looking character who insisted that we were all outstanding."

Mr. Tortosa smiled as he took their tickets. "Perhaps you misunderstood him, I think he said you were standing out."

Kim took over next, her tone serious. "Mr. Tortosa, we need to talk with you about something important that concerns the town's safety."

He immediately stepped aside and walked from the ticket line with the gang. Dion said, "We spent a day over at Lake Moon Glow earlier this week. The water was extremely high because of all the rain we've been having. Sometimes, the waves were splashing over the top of the dam."

"Really?" said Mr. Tortosa, "that doesn't sound too good."

Kim continued, "You know, with the earthquake, is there any possibility that the dam could have been damaged in some way?"

"I never really thought about that. It's unlikely, but you make a good point, especially since the water level is elevated. That puts extra stress on the dam. I will make sure qualified personnel have a look at it right away to verify its integrity. Failure of that dam would be catastrophic. It's not worth taking any risk. Thanks for bringing it to my attention. If it does need to be repaired, it'll be quite an undertaking. We'll need a considerable amount of heavy equipment and material."

The gang felt like they had done the right thing by informing Mr. Tortosa about the potential catastrophe, even though it seemed unlikely. They had no proof other than their deduction from images seen in Lucas's key.

Inside the festival, the mood was celebratory. As the gang walked through, they absorbed the atmosphere of rides and games, the smell of funnel cakes, and the sounds of upbeat music.

Anthony stopped at a food stand and asked, "Do you have a coveted bag of roasted peanuts?" The employee in the stand said, "They are not coveted, but you can buy some if you wish". He jumped at the chance, pulling some money from his pocket. He turned to his friends and said, "Would anyone like some peanuts as much as I do?"

Lost in his own mind, Lucas commented, "I hear familiar music in the distance." As the gang walked along, the music became more distinct. The same band of park musicians rehearsing every Saturday morning were performing on stage. The gang joined the small crowd and listened as they recalled the morning in the park when they first heard this band practice.

Just as their session was about to end, the band leader asked if there were any musicians in the crowd. Chelsea spoke up, "Lucas here knows how to play the guitar," as she raised her hand and pointed to him. The lead band member said with a smile, "Well then, come on up here and join us for our last song before the break."

Lucas was completely taken aback. He didn't think he was good enough to be on stage with the professional musicians, nor was he prepared to simply start playing on the spur of the moment. The crowd that had gathered around the stage heard Chelsea. They all began to encourage Lucas to go up on stage with comments like, "Let's hear you play," "you can do it," and "let's see you up there with the band!"

Lucas felt like he had little choice. He knew he had made substantial progress with his lessons, yet he had never performed in public before, aside from a friendly end-of-school-year talent show. This was a whole different level of challenge.

He sheepishly ascended the steps to the stage and exchanged a few words with the band leader. Then, all went silent. The drummer started counting, "1-2-3-4," and the band burst into action.

It was a simple song. At least, that's how it started. Lucas wasn't playing at the beginning, but halfway through, the lead guitarist unleashed some amazing licks and beckoned Lucas to join in. He held his own, much to the sheer delight of the crowd. His unorthodox fingerpicking style, combined with his incredibly fast fretboard action, gave the guitar a melodic tone that was uniquely his own.

When the song concluded, the audience cheered for more. Lucas hadn't felt that appreciated since he received his grandfather's key from his father. However, he wasn't about to risk damaging his moment of glory after having left a positive and memorable impression on everyone. With a slight bow and wave, he stepped off the stage to return to his peanut-cracking friends standing in the midway.

Everyone gave him a high-five, the whole gang left awestruck. Nate said, "You are a person of many talents, my friend." Chelsea had made a video of Lucas's performance and forwarded it to the rest of the gang, including Victor. He quickly responded back saying, "Lucas rocks with the best of them."

The rest of the day was full of games and delicious food. Several strangers came up to Lucas and shook his hand. At the end of the festival, they were all exhausted.

Before Lucas jumped on his bike to return home, he checked his key. Having been so preoccupied with the festival all afternoon, he hadn't gotten the chance to look at it. The last time he did was on the evening before.

At present, he saw a pin cushion and immediately thought of Lucia and how she had been struggling with decisions regarding her future life. As he turned the key over, the pin cushion became a porcupine. *That makes sense in a funny key kind of way*, he thought to himself. *Some people just know what they want to do early in life, while others don't figure it out till later. The important thing*, he thought, *is to remain engaged in all that life has to offer and put forth the effort required to achieve your goals.*

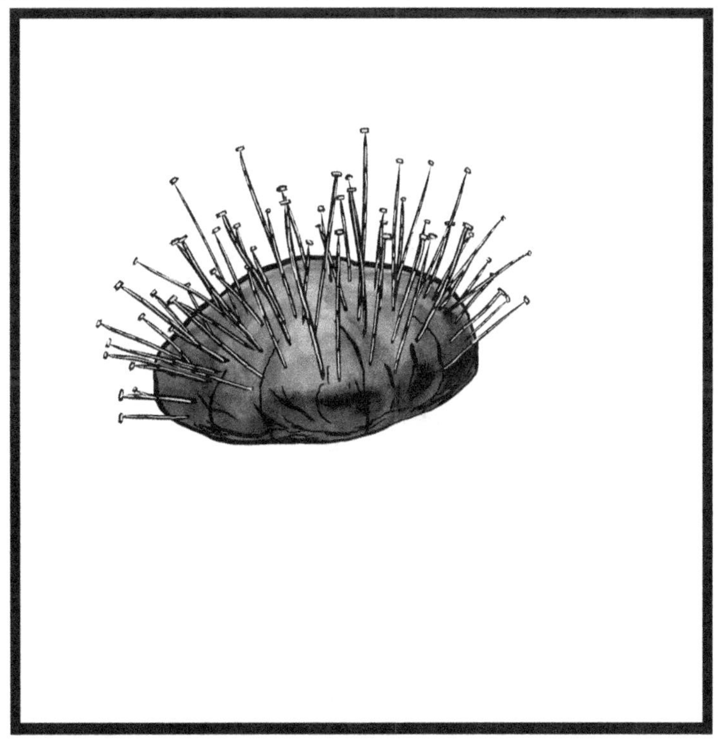

On his way home, he kept thinking about what Mr. Tortosa had said about the dam. Before entering the house, he couldn't resist the urge to examine his key once again. This time, he saw a harmonica. He thought to himself, *Well, at least my key is not fixated on water-related images.* Then, just as he turned the key over, he let out a chuckle. The harmonica became a bridge: not just any bridge, but rather the very bridge over the Wandering River.

There was something wrong with the picture, but Lucas just couldn't identify it. Then it occurred to him. The water in the river under the bridge was extremely high. Earlier when he and the gang were observing the bridge, the river water flowed strong because of all the rain. Still, one didn't feel as though if they were to lean over, they'd be swept away by the raging currents – but this was the image Lucas saw in his key.

What could this mean? he wondered. Then it occurred to him, *It means the dam has broken or is going to break, releasing all the water in the lake, which would, in turn, increase the flow under the upstream bridge.*

I am not certain this is the message, but I must tell everyone about this, he thought.

That evening, when Lucas was washing up for bed, his dad called him and asked if there was a soccer game scheduled for the upcoming weekend.

Lucas yelled back, "I will let you know in a couple of minutes." He checked the schedule and told his dad about a home game on Saturday morning at Sharefield Park. Lucas's dad said he would enjoy watching the team play and planned to attend.

Before bed, Lucas pulled the key out of his pocket and placed it on his nightstand like always. There was a bar of soap in the key. He laughed as he turned it over and saw the soap turn into an oversized truck. It was a cement mixer. He was not laughing anymore. Mr. Tortosa had said that if the dam needed repair, it would require heavy equipment. He knew the Lake Moon Glow dam was primarily composed of cement. He went to sleep questioning, "Is the dam going to be washed out, or is it going to get repaired before anything happens?"

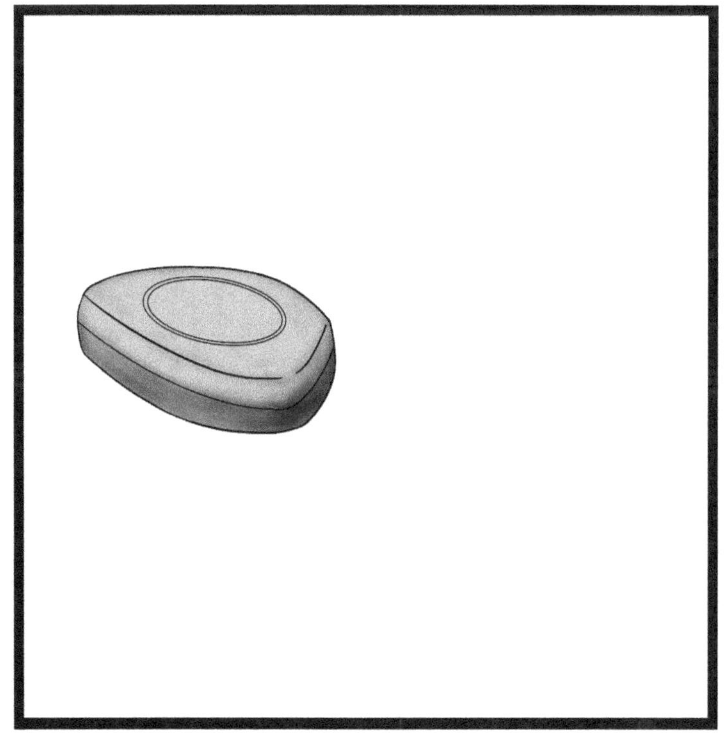

Lucas told Nate about the latest images he had seen in the key at soccer practice the following morning. The boys became more concerned that something potentially catastrophic was about to happen. Nate immediately explained the situation to the rest of the gang after practice.

Anthony said, "I hope Mr. Tortosa gets on this immediately."

Mr. Tortosa recognized the potential danger at the festival and arranged for a crew to evaluate the dam for damage the next morning while Lucas and Nate were at soccer practice. That afternoon, he called Nate and told him that time was of the essence. Indeed, a crack in the dam had been detected.

Mr. Tortosa said, "The responsible thing to do is to arrange for an evacuation of the part of Sharefield that would be at risk if the dam were to break."

He alerted the city officials, who instantly contacted the local TV and radio stations to broadcast the message to the city. The Sharefield Gang began to hear warning sirens and church bells, just like the day of the quake. The people on the east side of Sharefield were alerted to the danger and advised to evacuate because the dam could break loose. As Lucas looked at his key, he saw a plunger replacing the tower bell.

He said to Nate, "This does not look good."

Nate nodded in grim agreement.

Lucas glanced at the key again, hoping to see different, perhaps positive results, and saw a faucet transformed into a streetlight. He immediately thought of a flood and the damage it would cause. Then, it occurred to him there would be a total loss of power in the city if such a flood occurred. Water conducts electricity. The power lines will all short out. There would be no lights on the streets or anywhere else in the city if the dam were to break.

Just then, the rest of the gang showed up at the park. Nate sent them all a text message after Lucas told him about the image he saw of the soap bar that had become a cement mixer.

They stood huddled beside a fallen maple tree on the edge of the park, damaged by the earthquake, as they contemplated what might happen if the dam were to break.

Lucia frowned, "The entire east side of town would be flooded. People would have to get around in boats. Some could be trapped in their homes!"

"Let's hope everyone heeds the warning and evacuates in time," replied Chelsea.

"The problem is," said Anthony, "no one knows when, or even if the dam is going to break before it is repaired."

Lucas shook his head. "Oh, I believe it will happen soon. I keep seeing images that suggest the dam's collapse is imminent."

He pulled out his key to look, and again, he saw something strange. This time, it was a maple seed. He turned the key over and saw that it had become the ear of a person.

Lucas said, "This is so bizarre. We hear, we see, and we think. Now, it is time for us to act. What more can we do to help in this situation?"

Chelsea replied, "Maybe we should look at a topographic map of Sharefield and figure out exactly what areas will flood first if the dam lets loose."

Lucia agreed, saying, "This is a very worthwhile exercise. We could find such a map online."

Anthony pulled out his new Long Ranger and searched for the map. "This may not be easy to find," he said.

The rest of the gang all looked for the same information. Dion found it first and directed the others where to look on their phones.

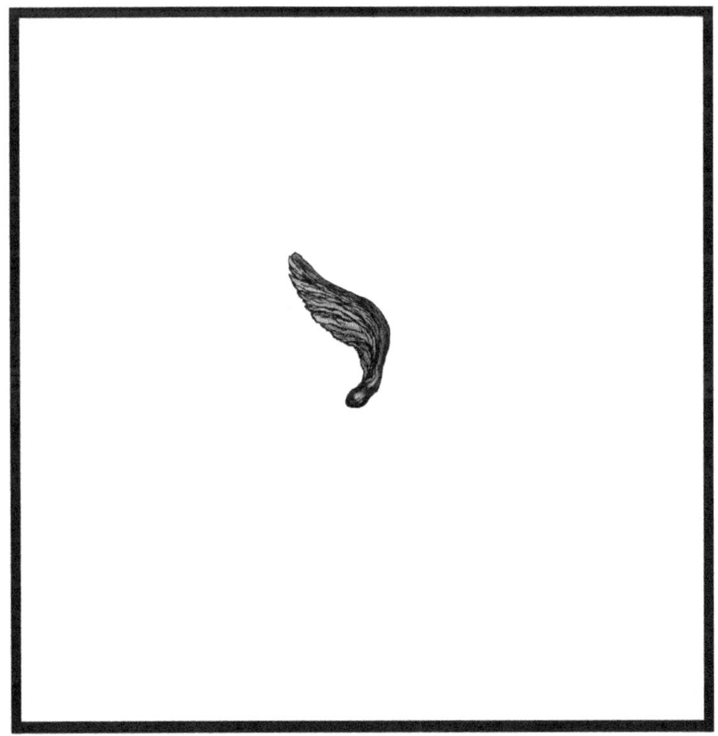

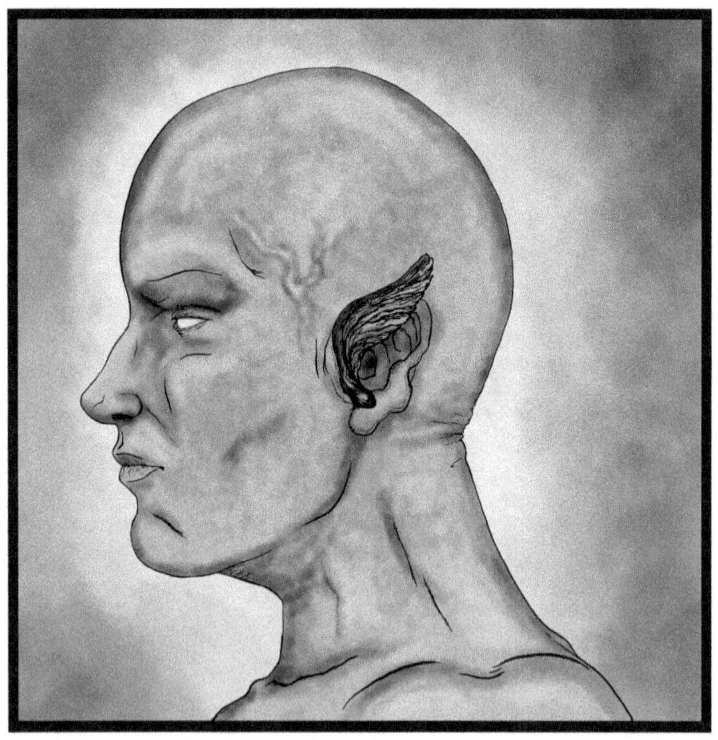

Kim said, "The east side of town is directly in line with the dam, and it is the lowest part of town, making it most vulnerable."

"Yes," said Lucia, "I believe there are already evacuation orders for that area. Fortunately for all of us, our homes are not in immediate danger unless it were to start pouring rain simultaneously, causing the water to crest beyond where anyone would expect. Kim, your house would be the first to flood among us, but it looks unlikely."

Nate replied, "That's good news, right? But what will be affected if the low-lying area just in front of the dam floods?"

Anthony said, "The big electrical power station is in that area, directly in the path of a potential flood."

"If a flood were to happen, it could knock the power out for the entire town," said Lucia.

Chelsea acknowledged, "That would be devastating for the hospital, even though it would probably not get flooded since it is up the hill beside the potential flood zone."

"You are right," said Lucas, who had spent a night there not long ago.

Lucia replied, "There must be a backup generator for the hospital, just in case of an emergency."

Lucas answered, "Yes, I believe that there is. I pass by an enclosed area, which could contain a sizable generator, every time I come into town on the bike trail from Diyton."

"What is the elevation of the generator location?" asked Kim.

"It's in a valley below the hospital and susceptible to flood damage," said Dion. "Evidently, when its location was chosen, the possibility of a flood was never considered. Who would have thought the Lake Moon Glow dam would ever be in jeopardy? We need to tell Mr. Tortosa about this right away. He will know what to do."

Nate said, "I will call him immediately. The sooner he is aware, the better."

As he made the call, Lucas took another look at his key. It showed a leaf, and the back side of the key became a canoe in a flooded residential area.

Nate no sooner picked up his phone to make the call than all the sirens and bell towers in town started sounding.

"It is happening," breathed Chelsea. "Right now! It is happening right now, as Lucas had predicted."

"The park is not going to flood first. We are safe here for the time being," consoled Dion.

Kim asked, "Is the route between us and the hospital back-up generator going to flood first?"

Dion shook his head. "It's hard to tell, but according to the elevations on the map, other lower-lying areas are going to flood first. We should have a clear path from here to the generator for at least a little while."

All of this happened within a few rings of the phone. Then Mr. Tortosa answered and said to Nate immediately, "We are in an emergency. Are you and the gang safe?"

Nate replied, "Yes, we are on the edge of Sharefield Park. We are thinking we need to move toward the hospital backup generator. It looks like it may flood, and if the rest of Sharefield loses power, that would be catastrophic.

Mr. Tortosa replied, "I believe all the residents in immediate danger have had time to evacuate to safer locations. The water is seeping through the cracks in the dam at an ever-increasing rate. The entire dam could break loose at any instant."

Nate said, "Well, if it does, it will wipe out the Sharefield power station and leave the city without power."

"Yes," said Mr. Tortosa, "I thought the same thing. That makes the hospital the top priority. I will leave now and meet you at the generator entrance."

Mr. Tortosa said to Nate. "I will contact an electrical power specialist immediately and have him meet us at the generator to figure out the plan of action."

Before Mr. Tortosa hung up the phone, he said, "There is no time now for gratitude, but thank you for the call."

Nate said to his friends in a direct tone, "We must start moving toward the generator, right now."

Lucas nodded. "I know the best way to get there. I travel this route almost every day. Follow me. It is not far from here."

The gang rushed along and soon arrived at the locked gate around the generator before Mr. Tortosa. Then, suddenly, the security light just outside the enclosed area flickered off. Immediately, the generator kicked on.

"It's happening," said Chelsea. "The water must have reached the power station; I hope this generator can supply the necessary power to the hospital to keep everyone inside safe."

Mr. Tortosa arrived a few minutes later. He said, "There were rescue boats out looking for anyone and their pets that the flood may have trapped. The water in some parts of town was already several feet deep. I guess you realize the power is out all over the city, just as you predicted."

"Yes," said Dion, "and the gate to this generator is locked. It just fired itself up before you arrived. I hope it's working properly."

As Dion spoke, a message came through Mr. Tortosa's phone stating that most of the hospital was operational, but there was one wing in the dark, and surgery was underway when the power was lost.

Nate said, "We must get inside this fenced enclosure and see if we can help."

Lucas pulled the special key out of his pocket and looked at it out of habit. On one side, he saw only a faint glow.

That is strange, he thought.

He turned it over and saw some convoluted combination of an owl and an alarm clock.

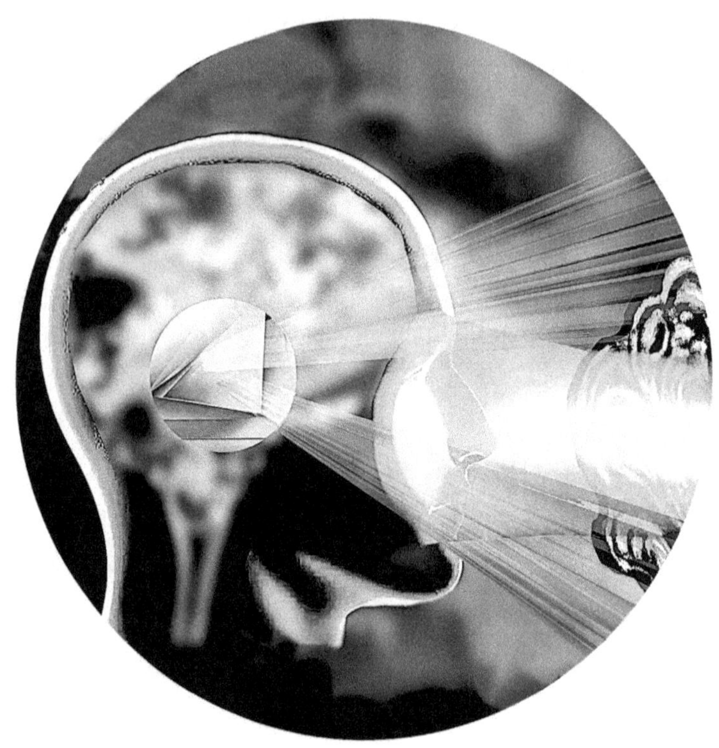

REFLECTION

Michael J. Piatt

He stood in front of the fenced gate to the backup generator, which had increased RPMs to full speed. There was a smell of mixed fuel and oil in the air as the generator was grinding away with ever-increasing white noise reaching the intensity of a jet engine on the tarmac.

Suddenly, the lock opened on its own, and the tall chain link door swung inside.

"How could this even be possible," yelled Lucas. "I did not even try to put my key into the lock. It just opened."

"We will worry about that later," said Mr. Tortosa. "Let's see if we can figure out why that one hospital wing is without power. They can't continue the operation in the dark and without the necessary life support. There must be a power distribution box somewhere here. If power is missing in only a portion of the hospital, there is a problem with a particular circuit."

Mr. Tortosa quickly identified the distribution box off to the side of the generator. As he opened it up, everyone gazed inside at the bird's nest of wiring and an extensive bank of fuses all arranged vertically in several columns.

"Look," said Nate loudly, "one of them is solid black. I think that one has blown."

"Good eye," said Mr. Tortosa. "I don't see any spare fuses in here," he said. "I am most concerned that the operation will fail in the dark. The message I received said that the patient could not be moved. I wish that we could do something."

Mr. Tortosa pulled the burnt fuse out of its socket. Lucas was standing next to him. The fuse was about the same length as the key in his hand. Inside the fuse box, the clamps that held the fuse on each end had pinched together, when the fuse was removed. Lucas knew that brass conducted electricity.

He asked Mr. Tortosa, "Do you think we could stick this key into the fuse socket to complete the circuit?" Mr. Tortosa looked puzzled. He was a surprisingly good handyman with standard fixup jobs, but he was unsure of what to do here.

Lucia said, "Brass conducts electricity about one-fourth as well as copper, but the key is thicker than the center of the fuse, so maybe it will work."

"We have nothing to lose," said Mr. Tortosa. He took Lucas's key and quickly flipped the big lever at the bottom of the bank, which cut the power to the entire group of circuits. Then, he rapidly shoved the key into the open fuse socket and flipped the power back onto the entire bank. "It appears to be working," he exclaimed.

Just then, his phone rang. The hospital personnel told him that there was power in the wing that was dark just a moment before and that the operation was proceeding.

Everyone breathed a sigh of relief as Anthony noticed that Lucas's special key was glowing on one tip and slowly melting before their very eyes from all the heat generated by the high current flowing through it.

He pointed to it and said, "Look, Mr. Tortosa, it is melting."

Mr. Tortosa remarked, "This won't last long."

The hospital administrator and a certified high voltage technician showed up at that time. The professional quickly put on special gloves and exchanged the melting key with the proper fuse, restoring power to the hospital wing without missing a beat.

A few minutes passed, although it seemed much longer to the gang, when a second call came in. This one was to the administrator of the hospital. The surgery had been completed with little additional complication. It was deemed a success. Mr. Tortosa told the gang, "That key and your quick thinking was instrumental in saving the patient's life."

The hospital administrator added, "Any long-term power outage during such a critical procedure would have been catastrophic."

The hospital administrator said to the gang, "You have done an outstanding service to the hospital and the whole city here today."

Mr. Tortosa agreed and thanked each one of them individually. Then he asked, "How could you have even known to suggest that all of this could happen?"

The hospital administrator added, "How did you manage to get into this locked transformer site? I have the only key, and it has multiple security features."

"The door just opened," grinned Lucas, "what can we say."

15

THE KEY'S MAGIC

After the key had cooled down, the technician returned it to Lucas. Then, the men turned and hurriedly walked away. Talking over his shoulder, the technician said, "A report that just came in says that the water has crested. The lower areas of the town are all flooded. We need to restore power to the town as soon as possible."

Mr. Tortosa responded, "Do we have information on how extensive the flooding is?"

"Yes," replied the technician, "the area extends from Lexington Street to the west, over to Clairmont on the east side of town, and past Elmwood south of the dam, almost to Ludlow."

That area was surprisingly close to the gang's predictions based on their view of the topological map. Beyond the perimeter of those boundaries, the elevation rose from the valley, making flooding less likely.

Lucas and the gang moved away from the generator to get relief from its deafening noise. Lucas examined his special key to see how much damage had been done to it. To his utter amazement, the partially melted key revealed some sort of circuit board in the center of the key and what looked like a very miniature video screen face.

"What," he exclaimed, "this key is electronic." He passed it around to the gang. Everyone looking at the key could not believe what they were seeing. Anthony responded, "This is a smart key feeding Lucas information."

Lucia said, "It always seemed to know what we were up to. There is not much room on this key for a receiver or a transmitter, for that matter."

"We are missing some important information regarding that key-making machine at the Diyton Hardware store," said Lucas. "Now I am more determined than ever to get to the bottom of this."

Chelsea checked the local news on her phone. Residents were advised to avoid the flooded area, and rescue efforts were underway for a few trapped in the flood zone.

As she read the news briefing aloud, she finished by saying, "Well, I guess that there is not much more that we can do now in response to this catastrophe. We have accomplished what was necessary for this day." The gang held hands in a circle to thank and congratulate each other, then said goodbye and dispersed. Everyone went home with a feeling of accomplishment and gratitude for the safety and security of their home and family.

Chelsea sat on the floor with Grand Paw and Bongo that evening. They played together quietly. Her dad pulled a flashlight out of the drawer and lit a couple of candles so that they could see well enough to get around the house. Like the other gang members, she will remember the time they spent without all the modern conveniences powered by the electrical grid.

The following day was bright and sunny. It was reported that all those stranded in their homes from the flood were rescued by first responders who used boats to pick up the couple remaining residents and bring them to safety. Full power was restored to Sharefield by the middle of the day. The hospital generator had operated satisfactorily throughout the night, allowing it to continue emergency operations without incident. A baby girl was born that evening at the hospital under the backup generator support. It was named Kallan, a name of Scandinavian origin meaning Flowing Water.

Diyton, located upstream of the dam at Lake Moon Glow, was unaffected by the flood. Lucas wanted to return to the hardware store as soon as possible to discover the mystery behind his special key. There was more information there than was shared with him previously. As he approached the Diyton Hardware store, he saw people lined up outside the door to get in. Everyone who had suffered damage from the flood in

Sharefield was there trying to pick up needed supplies to recover from the flood damage. Lucas realized that this was not the right time to investigate his key. He sent a message to his friends. They decided to all meet up at Sharefield Park that afternoon instead.

The flood and the damage it inflicted on Sharefield most naturally dominated the conversation. The gang was thankful and amazed that no one had been hurt in the disaster. Mr. Tortosa had already issued a statement saying he would be an integral part of the reconstruction by supplying funding for numerous projects. Fortunately, Mr. Granzo and the rebuilding of the Mustang Pizzeria and the new bakery were not directly impacted by the incident. Later that afternoon, Nate received a call from Mr. Tortosa thanking him and the gang again for their insight, call to action, and heroism in dealing with the hospital transformer.

He said, "The person in the operating room was saved by their quick thinking. He was a guy named Jimmy who was related to one of the schoolteachers at Sharefield High. He is still in recovery and not fully himself, but he specifically asked me to express his gratitude to the Sharefield Gang. Somehow, he thought he knew you."

Nate smiled and said, "Yes, we all know him well. He has strongly influenced us to think the way we do. It is us who owe him gratitude."

"So, all is well," said Mr. Tortosa as he hung up the phone.

The gang turned their conversation to Lucas's magic key. "Who would have thought that this key contained some electronics," said Lucas. "I felt as if this key was special as soon as it came out of the key-making machine because it had a different face on each side. How many keys are like that? It never occurred to me that it could somehow be an electronic device."

Kim, recalling what happened in one of their virtual reality sessions, said, "Somehow, you should still have that key intact."

Lucas replied, "Well, I do. I have the replica my father gave me that was made from my grandfather's key. I will cherish it." He pulled that key out of his pocket. It had the new face on both sides of it.

Lucia said, "Let me look at that key. Let's make sure that it does not contain some funny circuitry in its center." She pushed and tapped on the middle of the key and held it at an angle to the light to examine the surface. "It looks like a solid brass key to me," she said.

"I guess we should have looked at the other one more closely." Chelsea replied, "I'm not sure, even today, that I believed it was only the key by itself creating all those images."

"Well, I am pretty sure now that it was the key," said Nate. "However, it is still puzzling. How could the key know so much, and why only Lucas could see the images?"

Lucas said, "I will be heading to the hardware store for answers as soon as the crowd thins out and the flood recovery supplies are in the hands of the customers that need them."

That afternoon, as Lucas returned to Diyton on his bike, he rode past the hardware store. It was busy at that time but not overly crowded. He decided that he would return to the store that evening after dinner. When he walked in the door, he was greeted by a young female employee. He asked if George was working that evening. He was not, so Lucas asked if anyone at the store knew about the key-cutting machine. The associate said she would get Ms. Dara to help him make a new key.

Ms. Dara walked up to the machine where Lucas was standing and said, "How may I help you?"

Lucas said, "I need answers."

Ms. Dara looked puzzled. Lucas pulled the partially melted special key out of his pocket and said sternly, "Look, what are these electronics in the center of my key?"

Ms. Dara did not know what to say at first. After reflection, she replied, "Tell me the story of this key."

Lucas said, "It is a long one."

She answered, "I have the time."

After Lucas went through the entire story she said, "Let me talk to my supervisor."

She left momentarily and returned, saying, "I had to get permission to share the following information with you. Since you have this key, you must understand it, or else you will continue to seek answers from other places, and we do not want that. We are standing in front of a complex key-making machine with a lot of technology built into it, much more than is apparent from the outside." She said, "It has two modes of operation, one for making standard key reproductions and one for ultra-security protected lock applications, such as the gate at a backup power station. What you have here is an early system malfunction that resulted from a strange sequence of events. A high-security kcy was made, followed by a copy of a standard key with the same outer shape. Then, there was a copy of another standard key of the same shape but with a different face and the same key cut as the previous key. This unlikely combination of instructions caused an error in the system."

"I find this is all quite interesting," said Lucas, "but I still do not know how my key was able to show me images and how it was able to know so much about me and my friends."

"Yes, I am getting to that," said Ms. Dara. "You see, these ultra-security keys have graduated levels of identity verification. The key cut itself is irrelevant because it remotely opens a designated lock based on verifying multiple other parameters."

"Like what?" asked Lucas.

"Before we get into the details, you need to understand that this information is sensitive. It could compromise other holders of such sophisticated keys if it gets into the wrong hands."

"I will be careful with whom I share the information," said Lucas.

"Very well then," said Ms. Dara, "let's proceed. "These ultra-extreme security keys must comply with five distinct levels of verification before opening a lock. Each key works only with the specific lock to which it is paired. Four security features assure that the key holder is the rightful key owner, and the fifth assures the key holder that the key is legitimate.

"Everything is controlled and monitored through a central computer system maintained by the key reproduction equipment company. When a key is produced, it is automatically paired to the user's cell phone. It must be a phone within three feet of the key reproduction machine. Our employees are instructed never to have their phones near this machine, just as a precaution. We did not tell them why. After the pairing, the phone of the key holder records and transmits all sound received by the phone to the central processing system. That system, in turn, analyzes all data received from the user's phone and creates relevant images based on the stored subject matter. Those images are transmitted back through the phone to the key during key activation."

"So, exactly what is the key activation time?" asked Lucas.

"Well, as stated, the key owner's phone must first be within three feet of the key. The key must be in the hands of the owner. A sensor for detecting touch is in the center of the key. If the center of the key is not touched, it will be canceled prior to activation. The system also requires the recent recognition of the voice of the key holder, received through the user's phone. This information is transmitted and further analyzed by the central processing system. Provided all three of these conditions are met, a relevant image, based on the audio recording history of the key holder, is sent and displayed on the key. If the key holder recognizes the image as familiar, they are instructed to quickly flip the key over to the other side as a final level of verification. A miniature accelerometer embedded in the key is used to confirm the key's rotation. Then, and only then, will it be paired with the network lock in the immediate vicinity, which will open automatically."Image recognition by the user is crucial. This prevents someone from trying to replace a given key with a counterfeit duplicate. We know of such cases. The user must have some recollection and association with the image shown, derived from previously recorded audio from their phone. The key images only last for a few seconds and then disappear. A key can produce only so many images before its miniature power source is depleted. The display is a very advanced technology. It is a high-resolution organic LED display specifically designed for this application."

Lucas replied, "So, let me get this straight. My key must be close to my phone. I must happen to have touched my key in the center, my voice must be recognized, and I must see an image in the key face that I recognize. If so, I turn the key over to open the paired lock in the local vicinity."

"That is correct," said Ms. Dara.

"So, you are telling me that my key was paired to the lock on the fence gate that surrounded the backup transformer at the Sharefield General Hospital?" asked Lucas.

"Unfortunately, or perhaps fortunately in your case, yes, it was," said Ms. Dara. "The hospital administrator made a registered key in our system for the generator enclosure lock the day you made yours. About an hour before, according to our records."

"The touch sensor explains why sometimes I saw images in the key and other times I did not. Why was I seeing images on one side that transformed into something else on the reverse side of the key?" asked Lucas.

"That is a very good question," said Ms. Dara. "These smart keys are supposed to only show images on one side. Somehow, because your key was made with two different faces of the same shape and with the same key cut, your key was inadvertently projecting images on both sides. Again, I tell you that this was an early system error that has since been corrected. Until recently, we had no idea that any key like yours had ever been issued. If we had known, we would have contacted you immediately. It is fortunate that this key, or what is left of it, fell into your hands and not those of another with malicious intent."

Lucas replied, "So I suppose the last image I saw was only a faint glow on one side, and the crazy combination of an owl and clock on the reverse side was due to a power source drain. The key's response was about to terminate."

"That is correct," said Ms. Dara. "Evidently, you used it quite a bit, and one side of the key was losing battery capacity just before the other side. This allowed only one face to project a hybrid image of the two sides. The mild glow on the other side was probably the light from the active side showing through."

"Let me ask you, Ms. Dara, does an independent light source have anything to do with the display? My key showed brighter images when light reflected off it."

"Well, yes," said Ms. Dara, "that is very observant of you. A small solar collector embedded in the key face enhances power and displays increased brightness when exposed to intense light. It helps the key holder see and recognize the image projected in the bright sun. Also, just so you know, the central processing system uses a random rotation that never allows the same image, or image sets in your case, to be displayed more than once."

Lucas said, "That explains a few things. Every time I saw an image, I tried to pass the key to someone else to look at, but it always disappeared."

"That is by design," said Ms. Dara, "and it is a good thing. Either the touch sensor detected that the key was momentarily not being held, or the key may have moved too far away from your phone. Perhaps, on occasion, a strange voice other than your own was being picked up. Any of these conditions would cause the image to disappear. Of course, they would disappear on their own in a few seconds anyway."

Lucas replied, "Well, for what it was worth, this destroyed secret key was responsible for saving the life of someone very dear to the students of Sharefield Central High."

"That is so wonderful to hear," said Ms. Dara. "I'm glad that you understand things now. Actually, we were expecting someone like yourself to stop by. We recently received a call from the central processing center and another from the Sharefield Hospital administrator about the situation. By the way, our faithful associate George was never made aware of the special capabilities of our state-of-the-art security key machine. He was not able to activate the security key functionality on his own. Your key was purely the result of a system malfunction that he would not have been aware of."

Lucas thanked Ms. Dara for sharing the ultra-security key details with him and agreed to treat this newfound knowledge with extreme care.

16

THE KEY'S TRUE VALUE

As Lucas later thought about all that had happened since he found Ms. Brock's key, he realized just how fortunate he was. Had he decided not to return the key that he found in the school hallway, he would have missed out on so many enriching experiences with the Sharefield Gang. Before he went to bed that evening, he looked at the shiny new key his father had given him to remember his grandfather. He decided to keep it with him in place of the magic key and realized that it had more significance to him and value to his family than any advanced technology, system failure anomaly key he could own.

The following day, Lucas rode his bike to Sharefield as usual on those summer mornings. That day was different. Soccer felt less relevant amid all the destruction caused by the flood. Everyone in town assessed the damage and began to put things back together again. In a direct but somber voice, Coach Newman announced to the team that the rest of the summer season would be canceled due to the town's focus on damage recovery. Lucas and Nate knew that it was the right decision. Some of the players on the team were directly affected by the flood. There was so much reconstruction to be done. Playing sports was less of a priority under these circumstances. Chelsea and Kim got the same news from their softball coach.

The Sharefield Gang met in the park later that morning under their favorite oak tree. Everyone was there. Lucia suggested that they go to the hospital to see how Jimmy was doing after his traumatic operation. According to a note from his sister sent to Kim, he was about to be released that afternoon. Everyone agreed that it was a wonderful idea to visit Jimmy.

Since they would not be playing sports the rest of the summer, the gang decided to donate their time to the parks system to help clean up and restore the area around Lake Moon Glow. They wanted to contribute to the effort. This was something that they could all do together within the solitude of nature in a place that they had come to know and love over the years.

Then Nate asked Lucas, "Have you learned anything about your mysterious key." Lucas knew he was to be protective of his newfound information, but he also knew that no one in the Sharefield Gang would pose any security threat if he shared the information with them. He had already decided to do so himself the evening before. *After all*, he thought, *each of them was an integral part of the experiences associated with that strange key.*

Lucas said, "I have so much information to share with you, but you must agree, as I have, to keep it confidential. We must protect it just as we kept all the insights revealed by the magic key to ourselves over this summer." For extra emphasis, Lucas said again, "I repeat that this information must be kept secret in the same way."

Everyone wholeheartedly agreed with a show of hands.

Nate asked. "Is it okay to call Victor so that he can hear your explanation as well?"

Lucas replied, "Yes, I trust Victor as I trust the rest of you. Let's call him." After Victor was on the phone, Lucas shared the information he had received the previous day. He told the entire story of the technologically advanced ultra-security key.

Afterward, Anthony said, "I understand why it is important for us to keep this secret." Everyone else shook their heads in agreement.

Then Chelsea asked, "How did the key know so much about what would happen? It was predicting the future."

"I don't really know," said Lucas. "Sometimes the key showed us images of past events or things happening at the present moment."

Dion said, "Yes, but so many of those images seemed disjointed to us. Although they ultimately became clues that helped us in various ways."

"This is true," said Nate. "I admit that it was some time before I believed Lucas was seeing the images in the key. I thought that it was he who was somehow imagining them. Once I was convinced the images were coming from the key, I was also surprised at how well it could tie things together for us from seemingly irrelevant topics."

The conversation about the strange key continued as they walked to the hospital to visit Jimmy, their respected friend and mentor. When they entered Jimmy's room, he got the biggest grin on his exhausted face. He was overwhelmed with joy at seeing the Sharefield Gang. His sister Jill was there with him. She and Jimmy greeted the gang with open arms.

After everyone said hello, Jimmy assured the gang he was feeling strong and ready to leave the hospital. He thanked them for all they had done to make this special day possible.

Jill said, "I don't know the details behind your saving act at the hospital generator. How did you ever know to go there in the first place? How did you know there was a great need to be of service at that ideal time and place?"

Kim took the lead for the group and answered, "We cannot share all the specifics with you, but we felt compelled to help once we got the idea that there could be a problem with the power at the hospital due to the flood."

Jimmy replied, "I think I understand. You have powers beyond your understanding. Your intellect and initiative can allow you to assimilate information from many sources to create more things and solve more problems than you believe are possible. The key is to believe in your own abilities and to remain positive, even when things seem insurmountable."

Jill replied, "Jimmy, you must be talking about the meaning of the key featured in the Sharefield school plays over the past couple of years. You are talking about the human spirit to explore, learn, and create."

"That is right, Jill," nodded Jimmy as he smiled. "The very operation I just had was successful through the valiant efforts of the Sharefield Gang. It would not have been possible, under any circumstances, only a few years ago. Advances in medical sciences and all human endeavors are made possible by young adults like you." His eyes shifted sharply from one member of the gang to the next as if to tell each one of them that he was speaking specifically to them. "You see, the next innovations will come from you, I am sure of it."

Then he finished by saying, "Thank you again for all you have done for me."

They all said their goodbyes as Jill and Jimmy headed toward the hospital exit.

On the gang's walk back to Sharefield Park, Dion said, "Well, Jimmy did not know the whole story, but he knew well enough without all the information. He was right about continuing to learn all we can for whatever comes next."

Lucas looked at his friends and replied, "I think Jimmy did know the whole story."

"No way," said Nate, "he could not have possibly figured out all that happened with your special key, and certainly, no one has told him about it."

"This is true," said Lucas, "but when you stop and think about it, the key only responded to inputs that it picked up from my phone. That means that I, and in most cases, the rest of you, were all experiencing for ourselves the same things that the key was reflecting back to us. So essentially, we did not need that key at all to have reached the same conclusions through its assistance.

It just highlighted and reminded us of what we already knew. There is no reason why we can't do the same on our own without the key next time. As Jimmy said, it is a matter of combining our unique abilities with the initiative to discover and to create."

Chelsea interjected, "Lucas, you have so much insight. I hope that I have the opportunity to share more of that with you in the future."

Lucia replied, "You are right, Lucas. The processes are the same, whether we are creating art, solving problems, inventing new methods, dealing with a social situation, or reflecting upon ourselves."

Anthony said, "Lucia, you are an artist at heart. I always look forward to your next creation."

Lucas pulled the key he received from his father out of his pocket and said, "It is not showing me anything new, but it is a good reminder of what I have already learned with the Sharefield Gang."

By then, they were back at the park under their favorite oak tree, where the gang had discussed and shared so much with each other.

Dion remarked, "We have all grown from childhood through experiences we shared under this tree. Maybe there is more than one 'Tree of Knowledge' as Victor seemed to understand."

"Yes, with branches that go off in different directions, just like us," smiled Nate.

Kim replied, "But they are all rooted on the same base of relations with our friends, families, and surroundings."

Lucas said, "It is time to leave." He jumped on his bike to return to Diyton. As he did so, he said, "Someday, I would like to own a motorcycle."

Chelsea laughed and said, "I believe that someday you will, my friend."

Then Nate yelled out, "Good friends always stay in touch."

And who was to disagree with Nate?

THE END

AUTHOR

Michael J. Piatt lives in Cincinnati, Ohio. He has two children and three grandchildren. After a career as a technologist and inventor, he shares lessons learned through this book.

If you were entertained or found value in this book, please consider leaving a review. It helps immensely.

Enjoy the entire Key Series. Visit www.piattbooks.com